CH00693592

# BROKEN LOYALTY

## BROKEN REBEL BROTHERHOOD: NEXT GENERATION

### ANDI RHODES

BLUE JOURNEY PUBLISHING

Copyright © 2021 by Andi Rhodes

All rights reserved.

No part of this book may be reproduced in any form or by any electronic or mechanical means, including information storage and retrieval systems, without written permission from the author, except for the use of brief quotations in a book review.

Cover Artwork - © Amanda Walker PA & Design Services

*For you, my readers. Without you, I wouldn't be able to bring the stories in my head to life and for that, I am forever grateful!*

# ALSO BY ANDI RHODES

**Broken Rebel Brotherhood**

Broken Souls

Broken Innocence

Broken Boundaries

Broken Rebel Brotherhood: Complete Series Box set

**Broken Rebel Brotherhood: Next Generation**

Broken Hearts

Broken Wings

Broken Mind

**Bastards and Badges**

Stark Revenge

Slade's Fall

Jett's Guard

**Soulless Kings MC**

Fender

Joker

Piston

Greaser

Riker

Trainwreck

Squirrel

Gibson

**Satan's Legacy MC**

Snow's Angel

Toga's Demons

Magic's Torment

# BROKEN REBEL BROTHERHOOD

## THE ORIGINALS

A person who truly loves you is someone who sees the pain in your eyes, while everyone else still believes the smile on your face.
-Anonymous

# PROLOGUE

## FINN

"Would anyone else like to share?"

I let my gaze wander over the faces of others like me. Their expressions range from those of denial to anger to bargaining to depression to acceptance. The five stages of grief all on display in one cramped room.

"Finn, we haven't heard from you in a while." Chris, the leader of the group, hones in on me. They always do. "How about you share your story, give some hope to any newcomers here today."

Hope my fucking ass. There is no hope. There's nothing but endless pain and suffering. But that's not what Chris wants me to say. That's not what these people need to hear. I may be firmly rooted in the anger stage with no chance in hell of moving past it, but that doesn't have to be their fate.

I press my fist into my thigh and massage my way down to my knee, or what used to be my knee. Thanks to a bomb, it's a titanium albatross that I'll never rid myself of.

I don't say any of that though. Wounded Warriors is my last link to a world I'm no longer a part of and I refuse to do

1

or say anything that could jeopardize it. So, I bite my tongue and force the words that everyone wants to hear past my lips.

"I'm glad you all made the decision to come to group. I think you'll find that the more you attend, the faster you can accept your injury and the changes that come along with it." To my own ears, the lie is obvious. Based on the intense looks from everyone else, they don't have a fucking clue. "It's been one year, four months, two weeks and three days since I lost my leg, but who's counting?" I chuckle, like I always do at this point, and then lift my pant leg to reveal my above the knee amputation. "Sure, at first, I wished I had died in the bombing. I begged and pleaded with every single doctor and nurse that came near me to finish the job the bomb couldn't. But they never gave up on me." I pause for dramatic affect. "And eventually, *I* didn't want to give up on me."

There are hushed whispers, looks of disbelief, and smiles of encouragement. The reactions are the same no matter what.

"I strongly encourage each of you to find a buddy. Talk to those in attendance at these groups, learn their story, their struggle, and be each other's cheerleader. You aren't alone. I know it feels like it. I know that you all feel as if you're the only person in the world who's going through it, like no one else could possibly understand. But that's not true. You are not alone."

The moment I finish speaking, Chris stands and walks over to me. He thrusts out a hand and I shake it. It's his thing. I don't get it. Hell, I don't even like it. But if it makes him feel better, I can suck it up.

"Well, that was certainly a message we all need to hear sometimes," Chris says. His face falls when there isn't an immediate response from the others, but he quickly recovers. "Now, as I told you last month, I am transferring to another state and will no longer be running these groups. But my replacement is amazing, and I know you'll love her."

*Her?*

Chris glances at the clock on the wall. "She should have been here by now and I hate to end it before she arrives. Does anyone else have anything they'd like to share? Any issues you'd like to discuss?"

"Yeah," the guy sitting in the third chair to my right says. "What do you know about this new person?"

That's a valid question but really? What does it matter what Chris knows? She's either got what it takes to inspire broken vets to not get wrapped up in self-pity parties or she doesn't. And quite frankly, if she's not a vet herself, I doubt she'll have what it takes.

"Her name is Isabelle Mallory," Chris begins. "I don't know much about her other than her experience is vast when it comes to trauma and she's excited to take on her new position."

"Perfect," another guy grumbles. "She's as broken as the rest of us."

"No, that's not what I said," Chris replies with a frown on his face. "Her trauma experience is from a professional standpoint, not personal."

And there it is, the proof that I'm right. She isn't going to be cut out for this. No way in hell she's going to know what to do if she's not experienced a traumatic event herself.

"Well," Chris glances at the clock again. "I hate to keep you any longer so feel free to leave if you want. I'll stick around for anyone who wants to wait on Miss Mallory."

The room empties out quickly but I'm hesitant to leave. Chris is a good dude. A little too upbeat and positive for my taste but he actually gives a damn about his clients.

"Why don't you text her?" I suggest. "Maybe she got stuck in traffic or something."

Chris pulls out his phone and turns it on. Funny, I think he's the only one that actually turns his phone off like the sign on the door says. When it's powered up, I watch as his fingers fly over the screen.

He holds the phone up. "Hopefully she responds." His cell dings and after reading the text, his shoulders sag. "It seems she got stuck in traffic. She's still on her way but likely an hour out."

"Shit," I say because it seems like something I should be upset about.

"I'm just gonna text her back and tell her to turn around. I have dinner reservations with my wife, and she'll kill me if I cancel again."

Against my better judgement, and again, because I like the guy, I offer an alternative. "I can stay."

"Are you sure?"

He looks so hopeful that no matter how much I want to revoke the offer, I don't. I even throw in another lie to sound happy about it.

"Sure. It's no problem. I don't have any other plans tonight." Other than a six pack of beer and taking my frustration out on my punching bag.

Chris stands and puts his jacket on. Next, he throws his messenger bag—a fucking messenger bag—over his head so it hangs across his body. What the actual fuck?

"Thank you, Finn." He sticks out his hand. He's seriously going to make me shake it, one last time. And I do, because it's *one last time*. "It's been a pleasure working with you. I'm proud of the progress you've made."

"Thanks," I mumble, uncomfortable with the praise.

He walks toward the door but before he leaves, he looks back over his shoulder. "Hey Finn?"

"Yeah?"

"Give her a chance, will ya? She just might surprise you."

That's the moment I realize that Chris isn't as dumb as he looks and I'm not as good a liar as I think I am. I can't help but laugh.

"Fine. I'll give her a chance."

Two hours later, Isabelle Mallory still hasn't shown her face. Well, she blew her chance. I turn off the lights and make my way outside to the parking lot. As I step off the curb, heading in the direction of my Harley, another bike whizzes by me, narrowly missing my damn toes.

"Hey asshole!" I shout. "Watch where the fuck you're going."

I keep walking and see that 'asshole' is now parked in the spot next to mine. I take in the Harley, with its matte black and chrome finishes and hate that I'm envious. It's a damn nice bike. Clearly custom and tailored to its owner.

Speaking of its owner, they throw their leg over the bike and when the helmet is removed, my jaw drops. Standing in skintight jeans and a black leather jacket is a woman. And not just any woman. She's a dead ringer for the woman I always envisioned on my arm through life... before I was blown to hell by a bomb and one leg short.

She shakes her head and finger combs her long blonde hair. Seemingly satisfied that she's fixed her helmet hair, she whirls around and runs straight into my chest, practically bouncing back at the contact.

"Fuck, I'm sorry."

Not what I would have expected to come out of that sinfully sexy mouth.

"God, you must think I'm an idiot. I didn't mean to cut it so close back there." She hitches a thumb over her shoulder to indicate where she almost mowed me down. "It's just...I'm running very late, and traffic was a bitch and then I had the address wrong so that de—"

She slams her mouth shut and breathes deeply through

her nose. This does nothing to cool the boner that's forming in my boxer briefs. It's the first time my dick has reacted to anything since the bombing so I'm not even mad that I might embarrass myself.

"Let me start over." She smiles and even under the flickering light that supposedly makes the parking lot 'safer', there's no denying the way it reaches her eyes. "Hi."

She thrusts her hand out for me to shake and without thinking, I take it.

"I'm Isabelle Mallory."

*Son of a fucking bitch.*

## ISABELLE

"**W**hat is wrong with you tonight?"

I shift my gaze from the bottle of wine that Ruby set in front of me an hour ago to my brother, Isaiah. The concerned look on his face is fast becoming the norm for him and I'm finding that I don't fucking like it.

I tip my glass and let the burgundy liquid coat my tongue before swallowing it down. "Nothing," I say when my mouth is empty.

"Bullshit," he bites out. "You've been in a funk from the moment you walked into Dusty's."

"Isaiah, I really don't need your crap tonight. Can you please just…" I shrug. "Quit being my overbearing club pres and be the twin brother who leaves me alone?"

Isaiah looks over his shoulder and whistles, the sound piercing through the loud beat of the jukebox. Immediately, any Broken Rebel Brotherhood member present is making their way over to me, surrounding the stool I'm on like the cast of a superhero comic book responding to a distress signal.

I roll my eyes. "Yeah, thanks for nothing," I mumble.

I stand on the rung of the stool and lean over the bar, pulling myself across it so that I'm resting on my stomach and able to reach the bottle of Jose Cuervo I know Ruby keeps under the counter. I wrap my fingers around the neck and grip it tight while I scoot back to my stool. I pour the tequila into my empty wine glass and take a long gulp.

"You're gonna regret this in the morning," Isaiah quips. "Don't you have to work?"

At the reminder of my new job, I wince. And then I wince again because they don't know about the new job. They still think I'm working with my mom as a counselor for club members and their families. Guilt snakes through my veins. Shit, my mom. I haven't told her either. I chug down the rest of the tequila in my glass and grab the bottle to pour some more.

"Iz," Tillie pipes in as she yanks the bottle out of my hand and hands it to Isaiah. "What's wrong? You never drink like this, much less on a weeknight."

"Yeah, Isabelle," Lila agrees. "We're worried about you."

A very unladylike snort escapes my body and I slap a hand over my mouth.

"That's it," Isaiah snaps. "You're going home. Now."

I whip my head in his direction and glare. "No. I'm not."

"Yeah," Liam says. "You are. Isabelle, I don't know what's going on with you but whatever the reason for this little pity party, it'll look better in the morning. Go home, sleep it off, and—"

"I almost killed a man tonight!" I shout, unable to handle their worry a second longer.

"What do you mean you 'almost killed' a guy?" Isaiah demands. "What did he do?"

"I…" I hiccup and throw my hands in the air. "He stepped off a fucking curb," I cry like it's an offense that deserves punishment.

"He stepped off a curb?" Tillie repeats. "Like, he was coming at you and you were protecting yourself?"

I narrow my eyes as I try to imagine the scenario she described but a picture won't form. I shake my head. "No. He was just walking to his vehicle."

"Okay." Liam drags the word out, confusion clear in his tone. "Maybe you should back up a bit and give us all of the details."

I heave a sigh and stand. When I sway on my feet, Isaiah scoops me up in his arms and carries me to a booth. After he sets me down, he scoots in next to me. Tillie sits on his other side and Liam and Lila sit across from us.

I drop my head onto my arms. Maybe coming to Dusty's and drinking was a bad idea. Not only am I now in a position where they'll badger me until they've pulled every last piece of info from me, but I feel like shit. I lift my head and immediately regret the action.

"Can one of you please turn off the bar's spin cycle?" Bile rises up the back of my throat and I manage to swallow it down.

Isaiah chuckles. Actually fucking chuckles. "No spin cycle, Iz. It's all you."

He rubs my back and I wish I trusted myself enough to smack him away because it's annoying. It's also what he's done our entire lives. We may be twins, separated by mere minutes in age, but he takes care of me. He's a great brother and if I weren't so drunk, I'm sure I'd appreciate that fact.

"Iz, tell us what happened." Tillie's voice is distant, but I know she's not far away. I watched her sit down.

Without lifting my head, I launch into the story, the booze fueling my speech. "I was late. So freaking late," I groan. "I pulled into the parking lot and sure I was going too fast, but I was late. He was standing there, in the dark I might add, looking like some avenging angel sent to make all the troubles of my day disappear." I groan, remembering the flop of my stomach the moment I realized I was heading straight for him. "I almost killed him. I came way too close to running over his toes!" I wail.

"Wait," Liam says, and I can hear the laughter he's trying to hold back. "You almost ran over his toes?"

"That's what I said," I cry. "I mean, I coulda killed him."

Laughter erupts around the table and I manage to lift my head and glare at my friends. These people that I grew up with are supposed to have my back, not laugh at me.

"What's so funny?" I snap.

Lila is the first to calm down enough to answer. "It's just… girl, you can't kill someone by running over their toes. I mean, it may be hard for them to walk, but death?" She shakes her head.

"You know what I mean," I argue.

"Yeah," Isaiah says. "Yeah, we do. But maybe you should've led with you *almost* ran over his toes instead of 'I almost killed a man.'"

I wave my hands. "Tomato tomahto," I huff out. "That's not even the worst part."

"I repeat," Isaiah chuckles. "Maybe don't lead with 'I almost killed a man.'"

"Whatever," I snap. "Do you want to hear the rest or not?"

"Of course," Tillie says, smacking my brother on the arm.

"Anyway," I begin. "He was clearly pissed and yelled at me while I parked my bike. And then…" I shudder remembering.

"And then what?" Lila prods.

"I got off my Harley and he was right there." I feel my face scrunch up at the memory. "Like, right fucking there. I ran into his chest when I turned around."

No one says a word and the confusion on their faces forces me to explain.

I heave a sigh. "His chest, you guys. His very hard…"

Saliva pools under my tongue and heat infuses my system. "Very muscular, sculpted... perfect chest."

"Ah, now I get it," Tillie says with a grin.

"Get what?" I counter. "There's nothing to get. I ran into him and it was embarrassing."

"It was only embarrassing because you wanted to bone him in a parking lot after almost running him over," Tillie informs me.

"Well..." I tip my head back and squeeze my eyes shut. Fuck, I can't even argue with her. "Fine. He was sexy as hell and I wanted to apologize with my body. There, are you happy?"

"No," Isaiah says through gritted teeth. "I don't wanna hear that shit." He mock shudders.

I elbow him in the ribs. "You're an ass," I say with no heat in my words. "But I'm still not to the worst part."

"Oh dear God," Liam grumbles. "You are the worst when it comes to telling a story. Would you get to the point already?"

I look at all of them, silently praying for them to understand what I'm about to tell them. My decision to spend more time working with veterans wasn't an easy one, especially because I'm going to be doing it away from the club, but it's the right move for me. I love the club, my family, the life we've built. I believe in what we do, what we stand for. But I need something that lights my soul on fire and doesn't feel so... routine.

"Can I get another drink?" I ask, stalling but also needing a bit more liquid courage.

"No." They all speak in unison.

"Fine." I lean back and cross my arms over my chest. "I took a new job."

"You what?" Isaiah snaps.

"What does that have to do with your mood and what happened with this guy?" Tillie asks at the same time.

"I was late to my new job," I explain, maintaining my defensive posture. "I took a position with Wounded Warriors." When they all start to protest, I hold a hand up to silence them. "I'm not leaving the club, but guys, I need more." My tone takes on a pleading quality and I don't even try to hide it. "I need something I'm passionate about. And that's veterans. Sure, the club lets me work with veterans, but this is different. This is something I'm doing, on my own."

"Have you told Mom?" Isaiah asks.

"Not yet." My body deflates and I lift imploring eyes to him. "Is she going to hate me?"

"Ah, Iz," Isaiah says as he wraps his arm around my shoulder and pulls me close. "No, she's not going to hate you. How could you ever think that?"

"Because I'm not making the club my life anymore." Tears spring to my eyes and I let them fall. "I guess it doesn't matter. I probably won't last in the new job anyway."

"First, no one hates you for doing what makes you happy," my brother says with conviction. "That's all anyone wants for you. It's what we want for all of us. Happiness. Purpose. If the new job gives you that, great. And second, why don't you think you'll make it? It hasn't even been a day. Hell, it hasn't even been eight hours."

"That's what Finn said... that I wouldn't make it."

"Who the fuck is Finn and where do we find him?" Isaiah demands, sitting up straight and ready to walk into the fire without having any information. Being President of the BRB has really leveled him out, made him grow up, but when it comes to me, he still doesn't always see reason, only protection.

"Finn is the guy," I say.

"What?" Tillie asks. "Wait, Finn is the guy you almost ran over?"

I nod, my spirit crumbling inch by pathetic inch.

"Why did he say you wouldn't make it?"

"He said," I swallow past the lump in my throat. "He said that he knows I'm not a veteran and I couldn't possibly understand what they're all going through. He said that I'm clearly reckless and not taking the job seriously if I couldn't even show up on day one on time. So, not only did I about hit him with my Harley, but he's also one of my new clients and thinks very little of me."

"Fuck him," Lila grits out. "He doesn't know you, Isabelle. He was just mad that you almost hit him, and he lashed out."

"I know this might not be what you want to hear," Isaiah says as he shifts in the booth to face me. "He's a veteran, right? One who you discovered was coming from the group you were supposed to be at?"

I nod.

"And you said this is a group for Wounded Warriors?"

Again, I nod, not understanding his point.

"Iz, you can't take anything he says personally," he insists. "He's a vet with God only knows what trauma in his past. My advice?"

I narrow my eyes at him but nod. I always want his advice. He's the one person in my life who keeps me grounded, keeps me sane. He's the only person who can talk me off the mental ledge I'm on.

"Prove him wrong."

"How?"

"Show him that, while you may not have the same experience, you do know what trauma is like. Show him that, no matter what bullshit he throws at you, you can take it and you won't run from the challenge." He pauses. "Professionally. You won't run from the professional challenge."

13

I let his words sink in and the longer I sit there, the more I realize that he's right. I've never shied away from a problem. I've never been afraid of what someone has been through. Shit, I've spent my life jumping in with both feet and doing whatever it takes to help. I can do that with Finn. I *have* to do that with Finn.

"Okay."

"Great," Liam says. Something catches his attention outside of the booth and I look to see what it is. Ruby. "Now, it's almost closing time and you all need to get the fuck out of here."

I laugh at that. They've been together for a while now and every chance they get to be alone, they take it. I don't blame them. In fact, I'm jealous. I want that. I want to be so wrapped up in someone that it makes me forget reality for a while. I want someone to look at me the way Liam looks at Ruby, the way my brother looks at Tillie and Cooper looks at Lila.

An image of Finn pops into my head and I can't shake it away. No matter how hard I try to dislodge it from my brain, it remains, taunting, tempting.

*No. Absolutely not. Finn is a client. A fucking rude client.*

He's also the only man who's ever made me want to swallow my tongue.

*And the only one who's made you doubt yourself.*

I scramble out of the booth when I realize that they're all heading outside and, even though it's making me dizzy and nauseous, I keep shaking my head.

Finn is a problem.

*Finn is sex on a stick.*

Finn is off limits.

# 2

# FINN

*S*weat pours down my forehead and burns my eyes. I shake my head to clear as much sweat as possible but otherwise, ignore it. My muscles ache from exertion but I don't dare stop beating the shit out of the punching bag hanging from the ceiling. It's the only thing keeping me relatively sane.

My interaction with Isabelle Mallory has been playing on a loop for two days and I need the memory to disappear. She makes me imagine things I have no business imagining, wanting things that are no longer a part of my path in life. Things that I always thought I'd have but are now... impossible.

Another twenty minutes and a searing pain races up my calf and settles at the place where my stump attaches to the prosthetic. Phantom pain. That's what they call it. I've had so many doctors explain the phenomenon to me and each time I want to scream at them that there's nothing *phantom* about it. The pain is real, and it'd bring me to my knees if I let it. Correction: my *one* fucking knee.

I hop over to the bench I bought when I got tired of dropping to the floor in a heap. My basement is sparse, except for the punching bag and bench and I have no plans on changing it. I like it this way. Bare, cold, only good for one thing. Just like me.

My phone rings from its spot next to me and I glare at it while massaging my thigh. It's face down so I can't see who's calling but it's probably my mother, again. She has a knack for calling at the worst possible moments, like when I'm too pissed off to deal with her worry. I pick up my cell and look at it, frowning when I realize it's not her and I don't recognize the number.

I let the call go to voicemail. I don't talk to people. Okay, so that's not entirely true. I don't talk to people unless I feel like I have to. At group, for example. I talk there because I don't want others to end up as bitter and utterly useless as I am. If I can tell a few lies and make them feel like there's hope then fine, I'll talk. I'll talk until I'm blue in the face, not meaning a fucking word that comes out of my mouth.

I rise from the bench, limping on the titanium prosthetic, and climb the stairs that lead to the main floor of my ranch house. I came to Indiana almost a year ago because it was about as far from Washington state as I could get. Staying there wasn't an option. My mom has always been a bit of a worrier but ever since my dad died and I lost my leg, she's a million times worse.

My phone rings again and I lean against the kitchen counter and yank it out of my pocket. I don't bother looking at the number before answering it.

"Can't you take a fucking hint?" I bark.

"Finn, honey." I wince when my mom's voice comes through the line. "Watch your mouth."

"Sorry Mom. I thought you were someone else."

"That's no excuse." I'm suddenly transported back in time and am a fifteen-year-old boy being scolded for speaking to my math teacher with an attitude. I mouth her next words along with her because they're always the same. "I raised you better than that."

"I know, Mom."

I roll my neck in an effort to loosen my increasingly tightening muscles. I don't dare say a word because I know she'd as soon hop on a plane to chastise me than she would to finish the job on a phone call. I love my mom and would do anything in the world for her, but shit, I'm thirty years old. I'm a grown ass man who doesn't need his mommy to tell him how to act.

*Yeah, cause you're doing such a bang-up job on your own.*

"Finnigan Walsh, are you listening to me?"

I roll my eyes, grateful she can't see me. She only breaks out my full name when she's really worked up about something.

"Ah, the phone cut out," I lie. "Sorry, what did you say?"

"I said," she begins with a dramatic sigh that only a mother can perfect. "When can I come visit? I'd like to see the new place, see you. Heaven knows it has to be better than that hotel you insisted on living in, but I'd like to see for myself."

"I sent you pictures of the house, Mom," I argue.

I did send her pictures, but they weren't of my place. Shit, if she saw where I lived, she'd invite herself to move in until she turned it into a home. As it stands now, it's just walls and a roof. I haven't gotten around to furnishing it, other than a used recliner, a very uncomfortable bed, and a coffee pot. And all of that was donated to me through Wounded Warriors. The only items I actually purchased were the punching bag and bench in the basement, a large flatscreen television that hangs on the wall and a few bath towels and washcloths.

"Those pictures don't tell me anything, Finnigan," she

counters. "Are you eating well? Going to all of your doctor's appointments? What about Wounded Warriors? How is that going? Do you have—"

"Mom!" I can picture her pinching her lips together at my tone. "What's with all the questions?"

"A mother worries," she says simply. "Twenty-two hours of hard labor—with no epidural, mind you— give me that right."

I know I should give in and invite her to visit. It would make things a lot easier in the long run. But I can't. I won't. At least over the phone I can keep pretending that everything is fine.

"I'd love for you to visit, Mom, but…"

"But what, Finnigan?"

"I've got so much going on and I'm afraid you'd be bored." Another lie. "I'd hate for you to come all the way here and then be stuck in the house by yourself. I'm rarely home. They've got me doing so many groups and events, helping new vets acclimate with their injuries. I'm swamped, Mom."

"Oh." She thinks that I work for Wounded Warriors, not that I'm only a client. I actually didn't tell her that, but I also didn't correct her assumption. "Well then, maybe in a few months when you get more acclimated."

"Yeah, Mom. That'd be great." I breathe a sigh of relief. I've bought myself time. I pull the phone away from my ear and look at the time. "I hate to cut this short but I gotta get ready for group."

"Just promise me something, Finn," she says, and I hate that I hear resignation in her voice.

"Anything Mom." Despite my lies, my actions, I love my Mom and hate that I'm hurting her.

"Don't let life pass you by." She sniffles. "I hate the thought of you alone, caught up in a past you can't change and missing out on a future that could change everything."

*Motherfucker! Does everyone see through my lies more than I realize?*

I rub the back of my neck. "I promise, Mom."

"Finnigan Walsh, I mean it."

I chuckle. "I know you do." I pause for a second. "I really do gotta go. I love you."

"I love you too, honey."

I end the call and set the phone on the counter. I snag a bottled water from the fridge and make my way to the bathroom to shower. After taking off my prosthetic leg and laying it on the floor, I sit on the edge of the tub and swing my other leg over to stand under the spray.

I could have bars installed to make my routine a little easier, but I refuse to do that. I don't want things to be different. I simply want to go about my day, do normal things like normal people do them. I've already fallen on my ass in the shower so many times, I'm becoming accustomed to it. Maybe one of these days I'll fall and crack my head open and that'll be the end of my hell on earth.

When I'm clean, I sit back on the ledge to exit the tub and a loud banging on my front door reaches my ears. I try to ignore it as I towel myself dry, but it doesn't go away. Who the fuck is at my house? No one knows my address.

"I'm coming," I bellow as I wrap the towel around my waist.

I don't take time to put my prosthesis back on. My only plans for the rest of the day are to lounge around the house and that thing is not comfortable. I hop my way to the door, muttering to myself the entire way.

I yank the door open. "Stop fucking—"

My mouth slams shut when I see Isabelle standing there, her fisted hand raised to pound on the door some more. Her gaze drops to my chest and then to my waist and then further down to wear the towel ends. Her gorgeous blue eyes widen and her lips part as she takes in the lack of an appendage.

Anger wraps around me like a warm blanket on a cold winter night. Anger is familiar. Anger is comfortable. Anger is exactly what I need to get through any interactions with her.

The filter in my brain shuts off as the fury takes over. My words drip with pent up rage and I welcome it.

"What? Never seen a cripple before?"

# 3

## ISABELLE

"*I*f you're going to stare at me, the least you could do is close your fucking mouth."

My head whips up and I press my lips together. The pain in Finn's eyes doesn't match the hostility in his tone and the fact that I'm having such a visceral reaction to both emotions is... unsettling.

"Why are you here?" Finn demands when I say nothing.

I tilt my head and take in the man before me. Not that I need to. The image of him when he first opened the door in only a towel is burned into my brain, seared into the gray matter with zero chance of disappearing.

*Why are you here, Isabelle? You had a reason for coming and it wasn't to ogle the half-naked homeowner.*

Finn steps back and grips the edge of the door. "You are without a doubt the mo—"

"Do you wanna go for a ride?" I blurt out, knowing that's not why I came here and afraid he's going to slam the door in my face.

"A ride," he repeats skeptically.

I force my eyes to meet his and ignore the pulsing

between my legs that won't quit. "Yeah, a ride." My gaze dips to the bottom hem of the towel before returning to his face. I dig deep for the courage I know is in me somewhere and push my next words out. "Unless you're scared."

Finn throws his head back and laughs, giving him a completely different vibe. One that's not so angry. When he sobers, the negativity is back, and disappointment lingers. "I'm not scared. I am, however, busy."

I lean to the left to peer around him and when I straighten, I can see his jaw tense. "Yeah, right. You're busy." I shove my hands in my pockets. "Look, I know your first impression of me was…" I shrug. "Bad. I just came to apologize. So, I'm sorry."

"Do you always make a point to go to your client's homes and apologize for things?"

"No."

"Then why'd you come here?"

I roll my neck, not at all certain of how the tables got turned on me. "I don't know," I answer.

"Yeah, you do," he counters, full of a cocky confidence that wasn't there when he opened the door.

I huff out a breath. "Fine." I square my shoulders and lock eyes with him. "You told me that I couldn't hack it. You said that I can't possibly understand what veterans with lifelong injuries are going through." The more I talk, the more tense I become. "You said that you'd bet a thousand fucking bucks that I won't last more than a month." My hands are out of my pockets and I jab him in the chest with a finger. "Well, I came here to tell you that you're wrong."

"Okay. Prove it." He crosses his arms over his bare chest and leans against the door jam. "And I'm still betting that thousand bucks."

I give a curt nod before turning to walk away. His stare is

burning holes into my back, but I ignore it. I manage to get to the curb next to my Harley before he stops me.

"Izzy." I glance over my shoulder at him, annoyed at his use of a nickname. "Have a nice ride."

With those parting words, he hops back and slams the door. I resist the urge to throw my head back and scream. Finn Walsh is beyond maddening.

I throw a leg over my bike and fire it up. The rumble beneath me is calming. It always has been. I grew up riding but when I was finally old enough to drive and get my very first bike, I felt like a whole new world opened up. I had a freedom that I hadn't known existed until that first solo ride and ever since then, it's been what I do when I need to escape, to relax, to reflect.

I weave my way through town and when I hit the rural backroads, I full-throttle it through the country. Open fields dotted with baled hay whiz past me in a blur. All of the frustration, all of the embarrassment, all of the lust that slithered through me when I was in front of Finn disappears and all I feel is alive.

I'm better than the woman he turns me into in his presence. As I navigate the curvy backroads, I can't help but think back on my life and how I was raised. I was taught to be strong, independent, full of life. And I *am* those things, and more. I'd do well to remember that.

My cell phone vibrates in my pocket and I pull to the side of the road to read the text. It's nothing important, only my mom asking me if I'll be at dinner tonight. I send off a quick reply that yes, I'll be there, but I leave out the rolling eye emoji that I'm itching to add. I get the same text from my parents at least four times a week and my answer has always been the same, even though recently I've wanted to avoid these dinners like the plague.

Family has always been the most important thing in my

life, both my biological family and my Brotherhood family. Lately, though, it's getting harder and harder to be in the same room with people who are disgustingly in love. I wouldn't trade any of them for the world but I'm sick and fucking tired of their happiness being rubbed in my face every minute of every day.

Before I even realize it, I'm pulling onto BRB property and I take a left. It's the long way to my cabin but it means I can avoid driving past my parents' house. When I pull up in front of my porch, I sit there for a moment, taking in the scenery that has remained the same since the moment I was born. Everything about it is comforting… and lately, a little bit suffocating.

I spend the rest of the afternoon going over my schedule for the next few weeks and coming up with ways to engage members of the groups I'll be running. After Finn's reaction to me, I'd be lying if I said I'm not a little concerned about how everyone else will receive me. He's right that I don't know what they've all been through. He's right that I have no clue what it's like to come back from a war and try to be normal. But he's fucking wrong about a lot too.

I *do* understand trauma. I *do* have empathy and compassion. I *do* care about the people I help. And I absolutely *won't* give up until he sees all of that.

"You need to tell them tonight. I don't like lying to them."

I glare at my brother as we walk up the steps to our parents' house. We arrived at the same time and Isaiah urged Tillie to go in without us, saying he needed to talk to me. To say that it's weird having my best friend married to my brother is an understatement, and it's times like this when I miss her being on my side the most.

"I never asked you to lie."

I step onto the porch but before I can reach the door, Isaiah grips my arm and spins me around. I take a deep breath and release it slowly, making every attempt to not lash out at him. He clearly didn't hear a word I said the other day when I told him I needed my brother and not my president.

"You didn't have to ask, Isabelle," he says, dropping his arm to his side. "I would do anything for you, you know that, but…"

I cross my arms over my chest. "But what?"

"We don't keep secrets in this family. You know that."

"I repeat, I never asked you to."

Isaiah heaves a sigh. "I give up." He steps around me and yanks open the screen door before looking over his shoulder. "Tell them about the new job or I will."

The door slams behind him and his angry footsteps echo off the hardwood floor. I stare through the mesh screen, into the living room, and count to ten. I was already planning on telling them about the job at dinner but now I'm second guessing it. Not because I don't want to and not even because I'm afraid of how they'll react. I'm second guessing because I *hate* ultimatums and Isaiah just issued one.

"You gonna stand there all evening or come in and eat?"

I shake my head free of my sour mood and smile at my dad. Micah Mallory has always been an imposing man and even with his graying hair and recent health issues, he still is. He pushes open the door for me and throws an arm around my shoulders when I walk through.

"Hey, Dad," I say and twist my head to kiss his cheek. My stomach rumbles when the aroma from the kitchen hits me. "Something smells good."

"Pot roast."

"What's the occasion?" Mom's pot roast is usually saved

for weekends or Sunday dinner at the club house. Dad looks at me a beat too long and I feel my insides squirm under his scrutiny. "Your twin lines are showing." I chuckle at the name he gave to the two wrinkles between his eyes. He only gets them when he's trying to figure something out or deep in thought.

His hand automatically goes to the wrinkles and he runs a finger over each one. "One wrinkle per twin," he says. "I swear they developed overnight when the two of you were born."

We both laugh a little and then the moment is gone.

"So, what's the occasion?" I ask again.

Dad guides me toward the dining room and pulls out my chair for me before pulling out Mom's. "We're celebrating," he finally says.

Isaiah, Tillie and I exchange looks, all of us clearly unaware of what there is to celebrate.

"Uh, care to elaborate?" Isaiah encourages.

Mom and Dad now look at me, their expressions answering the question. The tension leaves my body on a loud exhale and Isaiah and Tillie join my parents in staring.

"How did you know?" I ask.

"What?" Mom says. "That you got a new job?"

I nod. "Yeah."

"Who do you think recommended you for the job?" Dad responds.

Mom waves her hand dismissively and picks up the platter of pot roast and dishes some onto her plate. "More importantly, why did you feel the need to keep it from us?" she asks when she adds mashed potatoes.

I take the platter from Tillie when she hands it to me. "I wasn't keeping it from you," I argue. "Not really. I just…"

"You just what?" Mom prods.

I let my shoulders sag. "I didn't want to disappoint you." I glance around the table. "Any of you."

"Why the hell would this disappoint us?" Dad barks, his voice reminiscent of the many times he would get frustrated with me as a child.

"I don't know."

"Yes, you do," he counters.

"I just..." I take a deep breath and try to collect my thoughts. "You built the Brotherhood from the ground up. It's your legacy." I shrug. "I guess I didn't want you to be upset that I needed something else in my life. That the club wasn't enough anymore."

"Honey," mom starts and reaches across the table to grab my hand. "Your dad and I want you to be happy. Whether that's with the MC or doing something else, your happiness is all that matters to us."

"Sure, we want you to be a part of the club," Dad adds. "And you always will be. But there is absolutely nothing wrong with doing your part to help veterans. Hell, it's half of what the Brotherhood does."

"So, you're not mad?"

"Of course not," Mom says with conviction. "We're proud of you."

I lean back in my chair and relax for the first time in two weeks. The moment I knew I had the job, my stomach twisted into a knot and remained there until now. Then a thought occurs to me.

"Wait," I sit up straight. "You recommended me for the job? I want this job because I'm qualified, not because my parents pulled strings."

"Trust me, no strings were pulled," my dad reassures me. "I heard about the job through some of my connections and your mom and I thought you'd be perfect for it. I simply made a phone call to throw your hat in the ring. The rest was all you."

"Oh." I relax again. "Thank you."

"Honey," Mom begins. "You don't have to thank us. We love you." She glances at Isaiah and Tillie. "All of you. We'd do anything to make you happy. Besides, it wasn't all about you. It's about the veterans too. They need someone like you."

Tears spring to my eyes and I wipe them away before they can spill down my cheek. Now that I know my family doesn't hate me for needing more than the club in my life, I only have one worry left: Convince Finn and the rest of my clients that I'm as perfect for the job that my parents think I am.

# 4

# FINN

"*C*an I get you another drink?"

I nod at the bartender but keep my gaze trained on the bar top. When I pulled my Harley into the parking lot, it was almost empty. I thought this little hole in the wall bar, with the Dusty's sign lit up like a neon Christmas tree, would be a quiet place where I could drink my demons away for a few hours. And for the first hour, that had been the case but now the place is filled with rowdy patrons and the blaring jukebox is giving me a headache.

The bartender slides a full glass in front of me. "Here ya go." She stands there and her sigh is audible, even over the bass. "What branch did you serve in?"

My head snaps up and I narrow my eyes at her. "What makes you think I was in the military?"

She shrugs. "You've got the look," she says, as if that explains everything.

"What look?"

"That look that screams you've seen the deepest pits of hell and even though you're not physically there anymore, you are mentally. Hell is still a very real place in your head."

"Lady, you have no fucking clue what you're talking about."

I wrap my fingers around the glass she set in front of me and slide off my stool. I turn to walk away but only take one step before she calls out to me.

"I'm Ruby. Army vet." I stiffen. "And I know a lot more about that look than you could possibly imagine."

Without responding or acknowledging her words in any way, I continue toward a booth in the corner. I have to weave my way through the crowd of bikers, ignoring the glares I'm getting from several of them.

When I reach the booth, I slide across the wooden bench seat and set my beer in front of me. My eyes follow the condensation that slides down the glass to pool on the table. It takes me longer to finish the drink than it normally would but just before the empty glass hits the tabletop, it's snatched from my hand and replaced with another full one.

"Thanks," I mumble without lifting my head.

"You're new around here."

I don't acknowledge the statement. I'm in no mood to talk. Unfortunately, they don't get the message and slide into the bench seat across from me. That's when I lift my head and am met with the annoyed stare of one of the bikers who glared at me earlier. Still, I say nothing.

"And because you're new around here, I'll give you this one free pass." He leans forward on his elbows. "But speak like that to my girlfriend again and I won't be so forgiving." He relaxes and crosses his arms over his chest. "I'm Liam."

"Finn," I say, frustrated that he keeps talking.

"Was that your Harley I saw in the parking lot when I pulled in?"

"Which one? Seems like there'd be a lot out there that you would've seen." I shift my eyes to the rest of the crowd. "Lots of bikers here."

Liam chuckles. "Yeah, but I came with them. We're the Broken Rebel Brotherhood. We're here a lot."

"Good for you."

"Damn, Ruby was right."

"Ruby?"

"My girlfriend. She's the bartender that you disrespected." He smiles with pride. "Also the owner of this place and, like she said, an Army vet."

"Ah," I say because how the hell else am I supposed to respond?

"Like I said, she's right. You've got a fucking chip on your shoulder and that look in your eyes."

"So she said."

"I've got news for you, man." He pauses and I begin to wonder if he's going to keep me hanging in suspense for his 'news'. "You're not the only one in here who's seen Hell and come out the other side." He slides out of the booth and taps the table. "Be glad you came out the other side at all." With that, he walks away.

*What the fuck does he know?"*

I nurse the beer that Liam brought me, not wanting to risk needing another and having to interact with someone to get it. Who the hell does he think he is, judging me based on my look or sizing me up by one witnessed interaction?

As I take the last pull from my glass, I slide out of the booth and the hairs on the back of my neck stand up. I was so lost in my own misery that I missed the shift in the atmosphere around me. The bikers have stopped talking and they're all shifting toward a group of guys harassing a young woman at a table in the opposite corner.

I can't hear anything the guys are saying over the music, but it's clear by the hunch in her shoulders and the way she wrapped her arms around herself that they're making her uncomfortable. When she stands up and tries to step around them, things take an ugly turn.

Everything seems to happen in slow motion. Liam and his crew jump in just as one of the guys pulls his arm back to hit her and an all-out bar brawl ensues. The pain that's always present disappears and I lunge toward the chaos just in time to stop a chair from bouncing off some biker's head.

I envision each person as my punching bag and land blow after blow into faces, hoping that I don't mistake one of the good guys for one of the bad. My knuckles are bleeding, the crimson dripping to the floor, taking all of my rage with it. The fight does more to cleanse my demons than any amount of alcohol could do.

"Motherfucker!"

I whirl around toward the yell and barely manage to jump back and avoid a knife aimed for my gut. Each time it's thrust in my direction, I block the blade and gain a few slices to my arms. They sting but my adrenaline is pumping and masking the sensation.

I keep edging backward until I bump into a wall, the man continuing to advance on me the entire time. Just before the knife slices into my skin again, there's a loud crack and he slumps to the floor.

I'm stunned by the turn of events and my eyes widen when I see Ruby standing there with a bat gripped in her hands.

"Looked like you could use some help." She winks and then turns to wade into the fray of others.

With Ruby and her bat in the equation, the fight dies down quickly. The guys who created the problem are all in heaps on the floor. All of them bleeding, none of them walking out of here on their own.

I look toward the woman who was their target and see her huddled in a booth, shaking like a leaf. I make my way over to her and the closer I get the more fear I see in her eyes.

"Are you okay?" I ask gruffly.

She nods.

"You're not hurt anywhere, are you?"

She shakes her head.

I glance around the bar to see if there's anyone else that could talk to her, someone other than a bitter vet with a chip on his shoulder. I'm not good at this kind of thing. When I see no one, I persist in making sure she's okay.

"Is there someone I can call? Someone who could pick you up?" When she doesn't respond, I continue. "You probably shouldn't be driving."

"I... I'm fine," she mumbles.

"Okay." I pull a chair out and sit down next to her, the pain in my leg returning and needing the relief. "Why don't we just talk for a few minutes, give you a chance to calm down, and then we can re-evaluate?"

She nods.

"How about we start with your name?"

"Ann."

"Good." I force a smile. "Ann, I'm Finn." I pause for a moment and then continue. "Can you tell me what happened? Do you know those guys?" I tilt my head toward the door where they're all being dragged out by Liam and his friends.

"No." She sighs and shrugs one shoulder. "Maybe."

"Maybe?" My gut tells me that it's more than 'maybe'.

"They're friends of my ex."

"Okay." I drag the word out, confused.

She fidgets with her hands and doesn't make eye contact when she responds. "My divorce was final two days ago. He was abusive and the judge didn't take kindly to that. I was awarded full custody of our son as a result."

"And I'm guessing he wasn't too happy with that."

She shakes her head. "He sent his friends to scare me because he knows that he needs to keep his nose clean if he ever wants a chance at unsupervised visits."

"We can help."

I lift my head to see Liam standing next to me, along with a few of his friends.

"How?" Ann wails. "I don't see how you can do what the cops can't."

"You'd be surprised at what we can do." The man standing to the right of Liam sticks out his hand. "I'm Isaiah."

She shakes it. "Ann."

"Nice to meet you Ann," he says and then pulls a card out of his pocket and hands it to her. "Here, take this. If you decide you want some help, call that number. I promise you won't regret it."

Ann stares at the card, squinting as if that will make this whole exchange make sense. Hell, it doesn't make sense to me and I don't have fear mixed in with the confusion.

"Uh, thank you." Ann stands. "I appreciate you all stepping in tonight. I don't know what they would have done if you hadn't." She shoves the card into her back pocket. "I really need to go relieve my babysitter."

With that, she turns and walks out of the bar.

"Cooper," Isaiah barks at the other man standing there. "Follow her. Make sure she gets home okay and there are no problems through the night. I'll send someone to relieve you in the morning."

"You got it." He walks toward the door and looks back over his shoulder. "Tell Lila I'll call her in a bit."

"Sure thing," Liam responds.

The door closes behind Cooper and the unmistakable rumble of a Harley being started is heard over the music. I glance between Liam and Isaiah, narrowing my eyes as if that will help me figure them out.

"Who are you people?" I ask.

Liam chuckles and Isaiah pulls another card out of his pocket to hand to me.

"The Broken Rebel Brotherhood," Isaiah says. "Pretty sure Liam already told you that though."

"Yeah, he did. But I still don't understand what the fuck that means."

Rather than explain, Liam says, "Thanks for jumping in tonight."

"I didn't do it for you."

"Didn't think you did. Regardless of your reasons, you helped and that doesn't go unnoticed."

The calm that the fight brought me has disappeared and now all I feel is cornered, restless, pissed off. I need to get out of here, get home and pound on my punching bag for a few hours.

I stand from my chair and turn to leave but Isaiah's voice stops me.

"Why don't you come by the club tomorrow? Address is on the card."

"And why would I do that?"

"Because Finn, you asked who we were," Liam says matter-of-factly. "And I hate to break it to you, but I have a feeling we're your people."

# 5

## ISABELLE

"*W*here the hell were you the other night?"

I lift my head from the paperwork on my desk and glance at Tillie. She came barreling in my house ten minutes ago and hasn't stopped grilling me about why I wasn't at Dusty's with the rest of them two nights before. The problem is, I don't have a reason, other than I wasn't in the mood to be with their lovey-dovey asses.

"I already told you, I got caught up with work."

It's not a total lie. I did do some work. Okay, fine. What started out as reading through client files to familiarize myself with the individuals I'll be working with turned into hours upon hours of staring at Finn's file and scouring the internet for any info I could find that might help me understand him better. But I'm sticking with 'it was work' and very necessary.

"Whatever," she huffs out as she sits down in the chair across from me. She throws her legs over the armrest and lets her feet dangle. "You coming to the clubhouse later?"

"Of course." I shove my paperwork to the side because I'm clearly not going to get any more done while Tillie is here.

"Do you know why we've all been summoned? I haven't had a chance to talk to Isaiah."

"You'd know if you ever quit working on your downtime." There's no heat in her tone so I know she's only giving me a hard time for her amusement.

"Probably, but everyone knows this new job is going to demand a lot of my time. So," I grin. "Play nice and answer my question."

"New case."

"Okay." I drag out the word. "Do you know any specifics?"

"It's the chick from the bar the other night. Name's Ann and she's got an ex who has fucks for friends. The ex isn't particularly happy with the custody arrangement for their son and his friends are extremely loyal... and stupid."

"Sounds right up our alley."

"Yep. I've got room for them at the shelter, but Ann doesn't want to uproot her son from the only home he's ever known. Isaiah wants to brainstorm other options to see if we can't keep her and the little boy safe without moving them." She swivels and plants her feet on the floor, leaning her elbows on my desk. "And he wants to introduce the new guy to everyone."

"New guy?"

This is the first I'm hearing of anyone new, and I don't like it. I know I wanted to do more away from the club, but I didn't mean I wanted to be kept out of decisions about who enters our family.

Tillie waves her hand. "Well, maybe he's the new guy. He's the hottie from the bar who jumped in to help when shit hit the fan. Liam and Isaiah liked what they saw and invited him to come check us out."

"What do you know about him?" I ask, frustration dripping from my words.

"Nothing really. I didn't get a chance to talk to him when

he was here yesterday. And a bar brawl wasn't exactly conducive to chit chat. But I can tell you this... he was fucking hot. If I weren't married to your brother, girl, I'd go after him in a heartbeat."

"Does he have a name?"

"Of course he does."

I stare at her a moment, thinking she's going to give it to me, but she doesn't.

"What the hell is it?"

"What?"

I reach behind me and grab the little lumbar pillow that sits on my desk chair and throw it at her. She doesn't even bother trying to catch it and it tumbles to the floor. We both start laughing and for a moment, I forget that we're adults with adult problems and lives and feel like we're fifteen again, talking about cute boys and sneaking out.

"His name, Tillie! What is his name?"

She shrugs. "Don't know. Never caught it."

I roll my eyes at her. "What good are you?" I tease.

"Well, your brother could tell you all the wa—"

"Don't you dare finish that sentence." I mock shiver. "I do not need to hear about my brother and you..." I shudder again. "Gross."

Tillie's phone pings and she pulls it out of her pocket and looks at the screen. She turns it to face me so I can see the text.

"We better get going before brother dearest gets impatient." I nod toward her phone to indicate the text from him. I gather all of the files on my desk and stack them in a neat pile. "I thought we had a few hours until we needed to be at the clubhouse," I grumble.

Tillie stands. "You really were in the zone, weren't you?"

"Guess so."

I don't know how the hours passed without me having a clue.

*Yeah you do. You were obsessing over info about Finn.*

I shake Finn out of my head and force my thoughts to the new guy. We need some new blood in the club, especially if I'm not going to be around as much. When my father started the club, it was small, but as time went on and one crisis after another darkened our doorstep, it became apparent that numbers matter. Things have been quiet for a few months but if I've learned anything, the quiet is just the calm before the storm.

Tillie and I head outside and straddle our Harleys. We could walk but neither of us like to pass up the chance to ride. When we reach the main house, there are no unfamiliar bikes or vehicles, so the new guy isn't here yet.

"'Bout time you showed up," Isaiah says as he walks out the front door and stands on the porch to stare at us.

"We're early." I smirk at him. "Granted, not by much, but we've still got two minutes before we're officially late."

"Smart ass," he quips.

I purposely hit him with my shoulder when I walk by and he chuckles. Just as the screen door shuts behind me, I hear Tillie and him talking in hushed tones and then the unmistakable sound of sloppy kisses. I ignore it and make my way to the library, where we'll all meet.

Liam, Cooper, Lila and Ruby are already in their respective seats and I take mine next to Isaiah's chair at the head of the table. My parents are also already seated, as well as a few of the other Brotherhood originals.

"We missed you the other night," Lila says after a minute.

"So I've heard." I chuckle at her. "Your sister's been pestering me about it all day."

"Yeah, she's good at that."

"Do you guys know anything about this newbie?" I ask,

letting my gaze move from person to person.

"Dude has an attitude." Liam shrugs. "But I think we're exactly what he needs."

"Attitude?" I ask, concern taking over. "Are we sure he's a good fit for the Brotherhood? We deal with enough shit, we don't need any from one of our own."

Liam waves his hand dismissively. "It's all good. I put him in his place."

"Besides, his attitude stems from the military," Ruby adds.

"He told you that?" I ask.

"Well, no." She shrugs. "But you can just tell, ya know?"

My mind wanders to thoughts of Finn. He puts off all sorts of bad-attitude-because-I've-seen-some-shit vibes. He also exudes sin which has me picturing him in lots of different—

"Are you all ready to get started?"

I lift my head to see Isaiah standing just inside the door, Tillie next to him. When they move toward their seats, my stomach plummets because standing in the space they just vacated is the new guy. Only he's also the man I was fantasizing about only seconds ago.

Finn's gaze lands on me and his eyes narrow. His eyes dart back and forth between my brother and me before he takes a few steps forward and stops again, seemingly uncertain.

"Have a seat anywhere and we'll get introductions under way," Isaiah instructs him, nodding in the direction of the empty chairs.

Without taking my eyes off Finn, I lean toward Isaiah and whisper, "What the hell is he doing here?"

"Huh?"

"Finn… why is he here?"

"He's a prospective new member," he responds.

"You've gotta be fucking kidding me!"

# 6

# FINN

"What is your problem?"

I rub a fist into my thigh to ease the ache. The moment I walked into the room and saw Isabelle sitting at the table, tension caused my muscles to spasm and seize. I came to the Brotherhood because I thought that there was something to Liam's whole 'we're your people' theory and after having visited yesterday, that assertion started to take root. For the first time since my world crashed and burned, I felt like I found a place where I could belong, a place where I could be myself and not be judged for being a dick.

Now... who the fuck knows?

"I could ask you the same damn thing, Iz," Isaiah retorts, anger coloring his face.

Isabelle crosses her arms over her chest, pushing her cleavage up and making it impossible not to notice the fact that she'd fill my hands.

"What the hell is that supposed to mean?" she demands. "I ask you to quit acting like my pres and be a brother for once. A brother who butts the hell out, mind you, and this is what you do? You invite the man who hates me and thinks I'm useless into the club?"

"Wait," I say, unable to stay silent. "Brother?"

Isabelle's head whips in my direction. "Yeah. We're twins."

My head falls back, and I stare at the ceiling. So much for finding my people. When I feel I'm calm enough to speak, I glare at both of them.

"I don't know what kind of shit you're trying to pull, but I don't need it." I turn to leave. "I'm outta here."

I walk out of the room, angry with myself for daring to hope that I'd found something good. I can hear Isabelle and Isaiah shouting at each other, but I don't even try to make out their words. They don't matter. Clearly I was right that I'm better off keeping to myself and I was dead on when I told Isabelle that she couldn't hack it. If my presence sets her off this much, there's no telling how she'd react to other vets and their problems. She's unstable.

"Hey, Finn!"

I look over my shoulder to see Liam standing just outside the door to the library. Curious to hear what he has to say, how he's going to dig them out of this, I face him, but say nothing.

"You're the guy she almost ran over with her Harley? You're that Finn?"

An emotion I can't identify curls around me, making me uncomfortable as hell. So, Izzy's talked about me? Huh?

He closes the distance between us. "Look, I'm sorry that you had to see that. They're not normally at each other's throats like this." He chuckles as if that explains everything. "Clearly there were some major wires crossed but no one was trying to pull anything over on you."

I cross my arms over my chest. "Okay. What's your point?"

"Just…" He takes a deep breath. "Come back in and give

us a chance." When I arch a brow, he quickly continues. "At least work with us on Ann's case. See that through and if you still want to tuck tail and run after that, go for it."

"Why would I do that? Why would I stay where I'm not wanted?"

He rests a hand on my shoulder. "Because I still think we're your people. And I think you need us." He looks over his shoulder toward the room we both left and then returns his attention to me. "Don't take my word for it, though. See for yourself."

With those words, he leaves me alone in the hallway. I feel like I'm standing at a crossroads. Go left and nothing changes. I remain alone and keep going through the motions of life because I have no choice. Or I can go right and everything changes. I find a new purpose, new friends, and maybe, just maybe, let go of all the bitterness and rage that is always present.

*Or don't turn at all.*

I go over my options in my head, again and again, until I find myself back in the library doorway. I didn't even realize I moved until Isabelle comes into focus. The shouting has stopped but the fury in her expression hasn't diminished and I feel my lips pull into a grin.

"Finn, man, I'm sorry about that," Isaiah says, garnering my attention. He glares at his sister. "Iz," he growls.

"Yeah, sorry." Her tone says she's anything but sorry, but I'll take it.

"I have no interest in being where I'm not wanted so if you're having second thoughts, tell me now." I say this to Isaiah, not really caring if Isabelle wants me here or not.

"No second thoughts, brother."

"Not your brother."

"Right," Isaiah retorts before sitting down. "Have a seat so we can get introductions out of the way and get to the case.

I don't like being told what to do. That's the one thing I don't miss from the military. But I take a seat anyway, if for no other reason than to get this over with.

Isaiah nods. "Good. Now, you know Liam and me." Again, he glances at Isabelle. "And Iz, obviously, but—"

"He doesn't know me," Isabelle grumbles. "He *thinks* he knows me, but he doesn't know shit."

"I know enough," I grit out.

"Oh, you think?" she counters. "Please, enlighten us."

I lean forward and rest my clasped hands on the table. "Fine. You're reckless and full of yourself. You think you can fix people, whether or not they want or need to be fixed, and it doesn't matter a bit to you that you have no fucking clue what they've gone through. You think your education makes you better than everyone else, experience and street smarts be damned." I pause to take a deep breath. "You're entitled and feisty and annoying and sexy and—"

I slam my mouth shut and avert my eyes. Judging by the stares aimed at me from around the table I've said way too much. And the fact that I'm already fully aware of all the ways I've put my foot in my mouth incites a rage within me that seems to be the norm when Isabelle is around.

"Well," Isaiah begins and then clears his throat. "Seems you know her pretty well." Several of the other members chuckle but it dies down quickly. "But what you don't know is that Iz is one of the strongest women I know." I lift my head to look at him. "Yes, she can be reckless." He puts a hand up to silence Isabelle when she opens her mouth to protest. "But she's not reckless with people or their trauma. She's smart and loyal and hard-working and crazy empathetic. Sure, she's not a veteran and doesn't know firsthand what you've been through... hell, what most of us have been through, but she'll be the first person to try and understand. She's someone you want in your corner, Finn. Always. Just because she doesn't fit your image of a Wounded Warrior or someone that can help you, doesn't mean that she isn't or that she can't. And this is all stuff you'd know if you'd get your head out of your ass for two seconds and give her a fucking chance to show you."

A hushed silence settles over the room and my stomach churns. A few years ago, I wouldn't have given Isabelle and her qualifications a second thought. Shit, I'd have taken it a step further and probably hit on her by now, tried to convince her of all *my* good qualities.

But now? I've lost a leg, I've lost friends, and despite the fact that I'm still breathing, I've lost my life. I may tell everyone else in my groups that they aren't alone, but they are. We all are.

*Until you're not.*

"Thanks, Isaiah, but he's already formed his... *opinion*." Isabelle's tone and the way her words drip with sarcasm tells me she didn't miss the 'sexy' part of my speech. "Let's just move on."

"Prove me wrong."

Isabelle's head swivels and she stares at me, her face impassive. "What?"

I shrug. "Prove me wrong. Everyone seems to think I don't know you. So," I lean back in my chair. "Prove it."

What I don't say, what I refuse to admit out loud, is I want to be wrong. Deep down, in the depths of my dark, cavernous soul, I want Isabelle to be all the things her brother says... and more. Maybe she can do what no one else can. Maybe this club, her family, can do the impossible.

Maybe they can bring me back to life.

# 7

# ISABELLE

"Can you handle this, or do I need to assign someone else?"

I scoff at Isaiah. He absolutely can make Finn someone else's problem, but he chose me. And he did it deliberately. Not only do I have the monumental task of proving Finn wrong, but now I have to prove to my brother that everything he said is true.

"I got it."

I lean on the railing of the porch at the main house and watch as Finn fires up his Harley. Our meeting ended a few minutes ago and, other than my brother and me, he's the last to leave. Finn sits there for a moment, seemingly looking in the distance at nothing in particular.

"If it's too much I—"

"I said I got it."

Isaiah puts his hands up. "Okay." He drops his hands and leans next to me. "I meant what I said, Iz. You know that, right?"

It takes me a few minutes to respond because I'm so focused on Finn. He pulls away from the driveway and points his bike in the direction of the main road. The way he handles himself, the way one would never know he has a prosthetic leg fascinates me.

"What do you know about Finn?" I ask.

"Enough," Isaiah clips out.

I turn to face him. "Yeah, but specifically, what do you know?"

"Like I said, enough." He rolls his eyes at me when I tilt my head to the side in annoyance. "I know he's from Washington state. I know he served our country and has some serious issues from that. I know that he's a good dude who isn't afraid to jump in and help people he has no reason to give a shit about." Isaiah looks out over the property and then returns his attention to me. "What don't I know?"

I consider not answering the question. I could cite client confidentiality and keep my brother in the dark. But if I step out of the role of counselor, I know I can't do that. Not in good conscience.

"Finn has a prosthetic leg," I blurt out.

Isaiah's eyes widen but only for a moment. "That explains a lot."

"You don't have a problem with that?"

"Do you?" he counters.

"No," I snap. "Of course not. But..."

"But what Iz?"

I shake my head. "Nothing."

"No, you have something to say so say it. You've never pulled any punches with me. Don't start now."

I blow out a breath, trying to come up with the right words to explain what's on my mind. "What if he can't hack it? With the club, I mean."

"Aren't you doing exactly what you hate him for doing?"

"No," I snap, too fast.

"Yeah, Iz, you are. I don't give a rat's ass about his leg.

Nowhere in our bylaws does it say members have to have all of their limbs." He takes a step toward the door. "Quite frankly, I'm disappointed that you're even making it an issue."

He leaves me alone on the porch, my heart splitting in two. I let his words sink in and am annoyed to find that he's right. And the only reason I'm making an issue where there isn't one is because I'm angry and hurt at the same thing being done to me.

I shake my head clear of my thoughts and pull out my cell phone to check the time. A quick glance tells me I don't have time to dwell on it because I have a new job to get to, a group to facilitate.

I also have to face Finn for the second time today and the only thing that's going to prepare me for that is a ride on my Harley.

I park my Harley on the opposite end of the lot as Finn's. I'm a little surprised he's here, which forces me to confront the reason for my surprise. I'm making assumptions again and I remind myself that I really don't know anything about him, other than what the internet told me.

I make my way inside and when I enter the room where the group is scheduled to meet, I force a smile. Despite my nervousness at the fact that they may all be judging me like Finn did, a calm settles over me. This is what I love. These are the people I want to help. This is my purpose.

"Hey, everyone," I say in greeting.

A chorus of 'hello's is the response. Some are looking at me skeptically, while others seem to be happy to have a fresh face running the group. And then there's Finn. His expression doesn't tell me a damn thing other than he's remembering his earlier challenge to prove him wrong.

"I want to start by apologizing to all of you for not making it to the last group. I know that I was supposed to be here to ease the transition from Chris. I won't give you excuses, just know that I'm sorry it didn't work out the way it should have."

"No one cares about that." I glance to my left and see a man grinning at me with almost childlike wonder. "We're just happy to have you."

"Well, thank you." I walk toward him and hold out my hand. "And you are…?"

He shakes my hand. "Shane."

"Nice to meet you, Shane." He grips my hand a little too tight and when I try to pull away, he gives one last squeeze before letting go. I chalk it up to the brain injury I read about in his file and dismiss the creepy feeling he gives me. I turn away from him and address the rest of the room. "Anyone want to start with introductions?"

"Why don't you share your background with us?"

I take a deep breath before turning my attention to Finn. He's deliberately goading me into a reaction, and I refuse to give it to him.

"Sure," I respond sweetly. "I'm Isabelle Mallory, as you all already know." I glance around the room. "I've got a master's degree in counseling and my specialty has always been working with people who have experienced traumatic events."

"That's an impressive education," Shane states.

"Thank you. I'm also a member of a motorcycle club. If you're from around here, you've probably heard of the Broken Rebel Brotherhood." I pin Finn with my stare. "I've served as a counselor to the club's clients, as well as providing assistance in the field, when necessary." I could go on and on about all the ways the Brotherhood skirts the line between right and wrong but that's not something we advertise. "I've helped victims of domestic violence, kidnapping, rape, child abuse, stalking… you name it, I've probably seen it."

Finn's eyes widen and for a second, I think he's impressed, but then he narrows them and averts eye contact. So much for winning him over quickly.

"Does anyone have any questions for me before we get started?"

When no one asks anything, I'm grateful. This group isn't about me and I'm bothered by the fact that Finn is trying to make it so. On the other hand, it gives me a tiny bit more insight into him. He enjoys making others uncomfortable, especially if it means that other's focus isn't on him.

"Good." I walk toward the only empty chair and sit down. "Now that we've gotten that out of the way, I'd like to just use today as a starting point. I want to get to know all of you. And not just what I can read in your files." I chuckle. "I've already done that. I want to know why you're here and what you want out of group." I lean forward. "So, who wants to start?"

Shane stands excitedly. "I will." When I nod for him to begin, he does. "Everyone here already knows me." He looks back at me. "Well, except for you Miss Isabelle. But," he takes a deep breath. "I'm Shane. I served in the Marines and did three tours overseas. During my last tour, I was shot six times. One of the bullets lodged in my brain and I've never been right since."

"And what do you hope to get out of group?" I ask.

"I don't really know." Shane's tone is sad, almost as if he's a kid who doesn't know the right answer in class.

"That's okay," I assure him. "Sometimes just being in the

company of people who understand what you've been through is all you need."

He sits back down, and I look around at the others. "Who wants to go next?"

When no one volunteers to go, I settle my focus on the one man I probably shouldn't single out.

"Finn, I'd like to hear from you."

# 8

# FINN

*I* have to fight a humorless laugh at Isabelle's obvious attempt at getting back at me for putting her on the spot. As much as I hate the move, I can admit that I admire her a bit for it. She's not a quitter, which is good. It's what everyone in this room needs.

*Including you.*

"I'm pretty sure you're the only one who wants to hear my story." I let my gaze roam around the room at the other vets. "They've all heard it so many times."

"Humor me," she says.

I take a deep breath and think about what I should say. Normally I give some stock speech about how getting injured is awful but it's not the end of the world. I talk about how life is good, no matter how bad my time in the military was. And I assure them that they aren't alone. Problem with that is that it's total bullshit. They don't know that, but something tells me that Isabelle will. Everything I tell them is a lie and normally, I wouldn't think twice about it. Why then, am I thinking about it three, four, five times?

"If Finn doesn't want to talk I can—"

"I'll talk," I spit out, effectively cutting Shane off.

He slumps back in his chair and crosses his arms in a huff. Shane hasn't been involved in group long, so I don't know much about him beyond what he's shared, but it's clear that the bullet in his brain has had lasting effects. He seems like a good dude, but he acts like a child most of the time. I can't help but wonder if he wouldn't have been better off if the fucker that shot him had killed him.

"I joined the military when I was eighteen. I'm thirty now so I served for almost eleven years before I was medically discharged." As I speak, I don't look anywhere else but at Isabelle. Even in the awful lighting of the room, I can see a luminous sheen in her eyes that tells me she's hanging on my every word. "My unit was assigned to take out a well-known organizer of a small terrorist group. We watched his compound for days and there was barely any activity, so we decided it was now or never. What we didn't know is that the lack of activity wasn't because it was safe to complete our task." At the memory, my stump aches and I try to rub my thigh to ease the tension, all the while, still looking at the woman who put me in this position. I shrug as if the next piece of information is no big deal. "I lost my leg to a bomb and the rest of my unit lost their lives."

"That's…"

When Isabelle's voice trails off, I continue. "That's life. It happened and I can't change it." Now it's time to dial up the bullshit. "I was enraged for so long, spending my days wishing that I'd died along with the rest of them." I finally shift my focus away from Isabelle, unable to take the sad, pitying look in her eyes. "Fortunately, I had some amazing doctors and nurses who didn't give up on me. I made peace with what happened to me and you all will too."

I stand up and lift my pant leg to expose the titanium prosthetic. "I live with this every single day, but it hasn't slowed me down. Sure, I do things a bit differently than I did before. My world isn't the same as it was but that's okay. The moment I realized that I'm not alone in this fight is the moment that I remembered that life is meant to be lived. Whether you've gotten to that point or not yet doesn't matter. You will. It does get better, easier. All you have to do is take a look around you and you'll see that. And if you still need more time to get to that point, that's okay. We're in this together."

I have to swallow past the bile that rises up the back of my throat at the massive shit pile I'm serving them. Maybe there's some truth to my words for some people but it's not the case for me. I hope it is for them.

When I sit back down, I rub my thigh like I always do. I don't look at her, but I can feel Isabelle's eyes on me, burning a hole through my skin.

"You're like the Terminator." I lift my head and narrow my eyes at Shane, trying to remember that it isn't his fault that he's got no filter. "How can life be better when you don't even have all your parts?"

"Shane!" Isabelle admonishes.

She appears to be the only one affected by his comment, as the others are trying not to laugh. I manage to hold back my own laughter, not even a little fazed by his comparison of me to a fucking robot. The Terminator is a badass.

"What?" Shane asks, his tone genuinely inquisitive and his eyes darting back and forth between her and me. "He always says the same thing and I don't get it."

"There's nothing to get," I say, annoyed. "My experience is different from yours and all of theirs. You don't have to agree with me."

Hell, I don't even agree with myself. But he doesn't need to know that.

"You shouldn't lie," Shane argues. "Especially not to her."

I bite my tongue. Why the hell shouldn't I lie to her? Or anyone else for that matter? I lie to myself all the time and I'm no worse off because of it.

"Does anyone else want to share?" Isabelle asks as she rises from her chair. She glances toward the clock on the wall and her shoulders slump as if she's relieved. "Well, it looks like that's our time for the afternoon. We'll pick up where we left off next week."

The attendees start shuffling out. The only one, other than me, who stays behind is Shane. He's watching Isabelle as she gathers her belongings and there's something about the way he's focused on her that rubs me the wrong way. I walk over and stand in front of her to block his view.

"You heading home, Shane?" I ask.

He looks up at me. "Yeah. In a minute."

As if I'm not even here, he stands and steps around me to walk up behind Isabelle. He taps her on the shoulder, and she whirls around, a startled look on her face.

"Oh," she breathes. "You scared me."

"Sorry Miss Isabelle." Shane shuffles his feet. "Um, I was wondering, do you want to grab a drink with me?"

She beams a smile at him. I have no interest in hearing her response, so I walk out of the room and toward the parking lot. When I'm outside, I start in the direction of my Harley but veer to the opposite end of the lot to stand by hers.

I want to go home and crash for a few hours, but I can't. Isaiah wants Ann watched and apparently, he thought it would be a good idea if Isabelle and I took tonight's shift together. I'm stuck with her.

*Maybe it won't be so bad.*

Before I can entertain an argument with myself, Isabelle walks out the door, Shane on her heels. I clench and unclench my fists at my sides. I don't want to be alone with her but it's becoming clear that I also don't like it when other men show interest, no matter how harmless it might be.

"What are you doing?" Shane asks when they get within earshot.

"Nothing." I glance at Isabelle in an effort to gage how much I can say. When she gives an almost imperceptible shake of her head, I continue. "Just wanted to ask her something."

He turns to her. "Miss Isabelle?"

"It's fine, Shane." She rests her hand on his arm. The gesture is innocent but Shane's face lights up and my blood burns. "Thank you for walking me out."

Shane hesitates for a few long seconds before he leans toward her, eyes closed and lips puckered to kiss her cheek. She seems to sense what he's going to do and steps away. Shane's face falls but he quickly recovers and walks away without another word.

We watch him get into the passenger side of a tan Buick Century. I squint to try and get a look at the driver and see that it's an older lady. Shane's mother? Possibly... probably.

"You ready?"

I shake away any thoughts of Shane and turn to face Isabelle. Am I ready? To spend what I know will feel like endless hours in close quarters with her? Fuck no.

"Yeah."

"We need to go back to the main house and swap out vehicles," she says as she puts her helmet on. "Can't exactly sit outside Ann's house on our Harley's and not be noticed."

"We can take my car." When she opens her mouth to protest, I don't give her a chance. "My house is closer. I'm sure Jace and Noah will appreciate being relieved sooner rather than later."

She appears to think about this and then nods. "Fine. I'll follow you."

I grin, inexplicably pleased with her easy acceptance. It also doesn't hurt that it feels like she just issued me a challenge. Challenge accepted.

"Try to keep up, Izzy."

# 9

## ISABELLE

"Where the hell are you putting all that food?"

Ignoring Finn's question, I lick the taco sauce off my hand and take another bite of the hard-shell goodness I'm holding. It's the fifth taco I've eaten since we arrived at Ann's and I don't even feel close to done. Finn ate three tacos and stopped but he seems to forget that he still has the nachos he ordered to eat. I don't remind him though because if he doesn't dig into them, I will.

I finish my taco and suck my finger to clean off the rest of the dripping sauce. Finn groans from the driver's seat and I fight to keep a straight face.

"This is gonna be a long fucking night," he mumbles and shifts as if uncomfortable.

I polish off another taco before tossing all of the trash in the Taco Bell bag on top of his container of nachos. I set the bag on the floorboard in the backseat and turn back around to get comfortable. He's right about one thing. This is going to be a long night.

The next hour is spent in relative silence, other than the music quietly streaming from the radio. There's been no activity at Ann's house, at least outside. The lights are on inside and I imagine she's going about her evening, blissfully unaware of her protection detail. Ann did agree to have help from the Brotherhood, but she also stipulated that she didn't want all of the details because, in her words, the less she knows the better.

The silence becomes deafening, so I ask a question that's been eating at me since group.

"Was he right?"

"Who?"

Finn doesn't take his eyes off of Ann's house and somehow, it makes this conversation easier.

"Shane," I clarify. "Was he right about you lying?"

Finn's jaw tenses and he rubs his thigh with a fist. He's quiet for so long that I start to worry he won't answer or that I somehow crossed a line.

"Depends on your definition of lying," he finally says.

I twist in my seat to look at him, incredulous. "What the fuck does that mean?"

"It means," he begins as he finally turns to look at me, "that if your definition of lying includes telling people what they need to hear in order to be okay with their circumstances, then yes, I lied. If you define it by actually providing false information about events that took place, then no, I didn't lie."

My head spins at his logic. Does he really believe the words coming out of his mouth or is he still trying to convince himself that he's not doing anything wrong?

"Lying is lying, Finn."

He quirks a brow at me. "Is it?"

"Yes!" I shout. "You're either being honest with someone, one hundred percent, or you're not. There is no middle ground."

"So, what do you call it when you tell a group of people

that you're trying to help and that you're part of a motor-cycle club that helps people but don't add in the fact that sometimes that help means coloring outside the proverbial lines?"

His words are like a blow to the face. I feel my skin heat at the implied accusation, and I hate that he's turned this around on me.

"That's different," I argue.

"No, Izzy, it's not." He returns his stare to Ann's house. "You told them just enough to make them comfortable. You told them what they needed to hear. *That's* middle ground. And it's exactly what I did. I told them what they needed… no more, no less."

I lean back in my seat, defeated. He's not wrong. There are things I choose to leave unsaid because it's nobody's busi-ness. I can acknowledge that, even if only to myself. But what I'm really concerned about is what he's leaving out of his story. What isn't he telling me? What part of his words are the lie?

Finn's sigh wraps around me like a heavy blanket. "I was telling the truth about what happened overseas."

I slowly face him, careful not to startle him into silence. "I'm sorry."

"Why? You didn't bury those bombs for us to trample on."

"No," I concede. "But I'm sorry that it happened. I'm sorry that you lost people you clearly cared about. I'm sorry you got hurt."

Finn continues as if I didn't speak. "No one in that group wants to hear about my sleepless nights, about phantom pain. They don't want to hear that I still wish I'd died along with the others or that life fucking sucks. They don't need to hear about how I go through the motions of every single day, bitter, enraged, alone or about my PTSD. They don't want to hear any of it." He glares at me. "I give them what they don't even realize they need: hope."

I swallow past the lump in my throat. Finally, I'm getting to meet the man behind the attitude and surprisingly, I don't hate him. In fact, he's even more appealing because he's being *him*. I reach across the center console and rest my hand on his thigh, ignoring the fact that his muscle bunches under my touch and the way he narrows his eyes at my action.

"I want to hear it."

"Why?" His tone is tortured, as if terrified of the answer.

"Because, like it or not, I care. And not just because it's my job." I take a deep breath and release it slowly. "And, whether you realize it or not, you're family. Or at least, you're close to family. If you join the Brotherhood, you're gonna have a whole lot of people who give a shit about you so you might as well get used to it."

"I don't want anyone's pity," he growls.

I let out a short chuckle. "Oh, trust me, pity isn't something you'll get from me or any of the others in the club. Quite the opposite." An image of my brother floats into my mind and I snort. "Isaiah is just as likely to knock you on your ass for thinking like that. We've all been through shit. You got hurt." His eyes widen and I hold up a hand to keep him from arguing. "Granted, it was serious shit, and you lost a leg but…"

"But what?" he asks when I don't finish.

"Suck it up, Finn. You were right when you told the others that they aren't alone. And neither are you. You got hurt, in ways I can't begin to understand, but that doesn't mean that you can't have a good life, the life you imagined. Hell, you ride your Harley like it's your bitch. Quit sulking and start believing the lies you tell everyone else."

I pull my hand from his thigh and settle back in my seat, giving him time to let my words sink in. Part of me is afraid that I've sealed my fate where Finn's concerned but it's only a small part. The rest of me knows that I didn't say anything that didn't need said or that he didn't need to hear.

Finn is a good man. He may be a disillusioned prick, but he's got more reasons than most. He doesn't even realize that the defense mechanisms he's perfected are there for a reason: to protect him from his fears.

*What the hell is he afraid of?*

"I'm not scared."

I whip my head in his direction, realizing I spoke my question out loud. I don't bother arguing.

"Okay."

He grumbles but I can't make out what he says. It doesn't matter. There's nothing he can do or say that will make a difference in my resolve to do exactly what he told me to do… prove him wrong.

What he doesn't realize is that, not only will I prove him wrong about me, but I'll also prove him wrong about himself.

Finn Walsh is a good man and it's about damn time he sees that.

∿

"Did you see that?"

It's two in the morning and I'm tired. We've been sitting in front of Ann's house for hours and there's been no activity outside the home. At eleven, Finn and I agreed to take turns catching catnaps and I just woke up from mine.

"See what?" I ask, groggy from minimal sleep and squinting to identify what he's talking about.

"There was a shadow at the side of the house."

I rub the sleep from my eyes and look again. There's one streetlight on Ann's block, making it difficult to see anything in the dark.

"I don't see anything." Finn opens his door, but I grab his arm before he can step out. "What are you doing?"

"I'm gonna go check it out," he says, his tone indicating that he thinks I'm an idiot. "I'll be back."

He pulls out of my grasp and steps out of the car. I immediately get out and jog to catch up with him as he weaves between houses and toward Ann's backyard. I was hoping this would be an easy watch-and-report kind of assignment but apparently easy isn't in the cards.

"Get back in the car," Finn demands when I'm next to him.

"Fuck that," I snap in a whisper.

"I've got this," he barks.

"I know you do but I'm not some fragile flower that needs a man to—"

I hear the shot before pain explodes in my side. I whirl around to face whoever fired the gun but my vision blurs as blood dribbles from the wound.

"Jesus, are you okay?" Finn asks, his attention divided between me and the phantom attacker.

"Yeah."

I hiss when he pushes my hand into my side to stop the bleeding.

"Here, put pressure on it."

When he's satisfied that I'm doing what he says, he takes off running, chasing someone who is long gone. I steady myself by leaning on the brick house and when I'm sure I'm not going to pass out from the pain, I make my way toward the street. As I'm walking, I lift my shirt to see that the bullet didn't enter my body, but rather tore through the skin and created a deep laceration.

Just as I step off of the curb to cross over to the car, Finn appears, seemingly out of nowhere, and falls into step beside me.

"We need to get you to a hospital."

"No, we don't. It's a flesh wound. A pretty bad flesh wound but I'll see Doc back at the club. He'll fix me up. Right now, we need to call Isaiah and have him send someone to relieve us. We need to get out of here before the cops show up. Someone is bound to have called them."

Finn opens my door for me and guides me into the passenger seat. He rounds the hood of the car and I catch a glimpse of his face in the glow of the streetlight. He's angry. Angrier than I've ever seen him. I can't help but wonder if it's because I got hurt or if it's because the person got away.

"Did you see who shot you?" he asks after he closes the driver's side door behind him.

I shake my head.

"It makes no sense," he says, more to himself than to me.

"What?"

I pull my cell phone out of my pocket and text my brother. His response is immediate, so I know we'll have reinforcements soon.

"We weren't even next to Ann's house. Hers is two doors down. If someone is outside of her place, a threat to her, how did they see us?"

I shrug. "Does it matter? Clearly we're not the only ones out here doing surveillance tonight. They've probably been watching us for hours and saw the perfect opportunity to make their move and not have it linked to Ann when we were weaving through neighboring yards."

"Yeah, maybe," he agrees.

"Let it go. They're gone. We'll get 'em... just not tonight."

The tension in his body doesn't ease. Finn is on high alert and something tells me that's not going to end any time soon. I shift in my seat and inhale sharply when my side screams in protest.

"Here," Finn says as he reaches across the vehicle and grabs the hem of my shirt. "Let me take a look."

I don't stop him when he lifts the blood-soaked cotton, exposing my abdomen. I don't stop him when his scrutiny becomes almost too much to bear. I don't stop him when his eyes darken and his grip on my shirt tightens.

"It looks worse than it is."

He reaches into his back seat and when his hand comes back into view, I see a white t-shirt in his grip. He folds the shirt into a makeshift bandage and presses it to my side. I grit my teeth against the pain but otherwise don't react.

"This'll help keep the bleeding in check."

He leans back in his seat and releases a sigh.

"Thanks."

"For what? I got you shot."

"You didn't pull the trigger."

"Maybe not but you wouldn't have been out there if it weren't for me."

"On the other hand, I could still be out there bleeding out in some random person's yard if it weren't for you."

His laugh is hollow. "You're going to argue with me about this until I give in, aren't you?"

I grin at him through the pain. "Ah, so maybe you do know me just a little. Now, can we please go before the cops get here? I'd rather not talk to them about gunshots and what we're doing here in the middle of the night."

# FINN

*Y*ou do know me just a little.

Isabelle's words run through my head in between little snippets of the hours before Isaiah sent me home. I'm surprised he didn't send me packing earlier but if I'm being honest, I wouldn't have gone if he had tried.

The punching bag swings back toward me and I execute a right jab, never allowing it to come to a complete stop. I replay the events of our 'assignment' and take out all of my rage on the red leather, as if it will change the outcome. Nothing can change the fact that Isabelle got shot because of me. No amount of punching will change a fucking thing.

For a split second after hearing the gunshot, I waited for the pain. I wanted to feel it, to feel the burning agony of a bullet tearing through my flesh. But it never came. And when I registered that, and the fact that Isabelle had stopped talking, my heart skipped a beat.

My blood ran cold when I saw the crimson liquid trickle from her side. I was torn between wanting to make sure she was okay and needing to get the bastard who'd pulled the trigger. She made the decision easy, or as easy as it could be.

As long as she was talking, moving around, *breathing*, I was going to do what I could… get the fucker. The problem is, I didn't get him. Not even a glimpse. Isabelle, her brother, the Brotherhood, they're all convinced that it was Ann's ex or his buddies. Me? Not so much.

*Who else could it be?*

My phone rings from the bench behind me before I can come up with any other possibilities. I groan, wanting to ignore it and knowing I can't. What if it's Isabelle and she needs something?

*And when the fuck did you start giving a shit about what she needs?*

The ringing stops and I listen for the ding that will alert me to a voicemail. No ding comes but the ringing starts again. I hobble over to the bench against my better judgement and collapse onto the wooden seat. I wrap my fingers around my phone and lift it to my ear.

"Hello?"

"Finnigan, it's your mother."

I breathe a sigh of equal parts relief and disappointment. Angry at myself for daring to hope it would be Isabelle on the other end flares.

"Hi, Mom."

"You don't sound happy to hear from me."

"I am," I rush to assure her. "Just trying to catch my breath from my workout."

"Uh huh." I never could lie quite convincingly enough to her, at least about some things. "Why aren't you at work?"

"Mom, if you thought I would be at work, why are you calling?"

"Can't a mother want to talk to her son?"

"Yes, she can," I concede. "Let's start over." I scrub a towel over my face to wipe away the sweat. "How are you?"

"I'm fine, Finnigan. But I didn't call to make small talk."

I chuckle. "Okay. What do you want to talk about?"

"When are you going to let me come visit?"

"Mom, we talked about this," I remind her. How many times do I have to tell her I'm too busy? "It's not a good time."

"And I've decided that I don't care."

My jaw tics and my muscles tense. The last thing I need is my mother underfoot. Not only do I not want to deal with the censure I'm bound to get for, well, everything, but I'm also not thrilled about the prospect of her getting caught in the crossfire of whatever the fuck last night was.

"Mom, just give me a few more months," I plead, fairly certain it's pointless. "I told you, things are crazy right now."

"Things are always going to be crazy, Finn." She sniffles and I feel myself begin to soften. "Life is crazy. And it's too short."

Instantly, I'm on high alert. "What's going on? Are you sick? Did something happen?"

She lets out a watery laugh. "No, no, nothing like that." She's hiding something, I'm sure of it. But before I can question her, she drops a bombshell. "I booked a flight for next week. I'll need you to pick me up from the airport."

My heart thuds and my mind races faster than any Olympic sprinter. I have less than a week to get my house in order. Less than a week to figure out how I'm going to prove to her that I'm fine and not still carrying baggage from the bombing. I'm not sure I can pull it off, but I know I have to try. For her.

"Did you hear me, Finnigan?"

I nod and remember she can't see me. She'd be able to if I would have agreed to teach her how to use Facetime, but I've refused because there were some things I didn't want her to see. Specifically, me. The broken, shattered shell of the son she knew.

"Yeah, I heard you."

"Will you pick me up? Or are you going to force me to rent a car?"

"I'll pick you up. When does your flight land?"

After she gives me the details, we finalize our—correction, *her*—plans. When I disconnect the call, I let my anger get the better of me. I lunge toward the punching bag and unleash all of my wrath.

I don't know how long I battle the leather, how many punches I throw, how many groans and shouts and grunts I expel, but an ache settles into my muscles, forcing me to stop. I'm tired, exhausted, *done*. I can't do this anymore. I can't keep pretending that I'm okay, praying that others won't pick up on the fact that my existence is a lie.

I reach out and wrap my arms around the punching bag to stop it from swinging. When it settles, I hobble toward the steps that will lead me out of my basement, snagging my phone from the bench as I pass. When I try to climb them, the consequences of my outburst hit me. I can't take a single step.

I turn around and plop onto the bottom tread, determined to get upstairs one way or another. I scoot up on my ass, one step at a time, and when I reach the top, I manage to slide out of the way enough that I can slam the door.

The sound of the wood crashing into its frame reverberates around me. I fall back onto the kitchen floor and stare at the ceiling. I have no idea how I'm going to get everything done before my mom gets here.

I close my eyes and make a mental list of things I need to do. I also try to figure out a way to tell Isaiah that I need to take a step back for a few days while my mom is here because I won't put her in a position where she's in danger. I clench my teeth at that thought. I don't want to take a step back. And something tells me that if I do, I might lose the connection to my people.

*And when the fuck did I start thinking of them as my people?*

An image of Isabelle sitting on the edge of the coffee table at the Brotherhood's main house slips into my thoughts. Doc was stitching her up and she barely flinched. Sure, the tequila and lidocaine helped but I've seen grown men about piss their pants at the sight of a needle so her reaction, or lack of one, was impressive. It's also the moment I acknowledged, to myself, that I very well could have been wrong about her.

A grin spreads across my face as I recall the hours at the main house, the arguments between Isabelle and her brother. Isaiah wants to pull her from Ann's case. He wants to protect her, make sure she remains unscathed, untouched. But she's having none of it. She may have stepped outside of the club to find more fulfillment, but she's just as dedicated to her family and their cause as anyone else. At least from what I've seen.

*You like her.*

Easing myself into a sitting position, I push that thought away. I don't like her. I can be impressed by someone and not like them.

*Fine. You wanna get in her pants.*

There's no denying that, even to myself. Isabelle is sexy as fuck and she's the first person who's been able to stir something up in me that I thought was long gone. Lust, longing... *need*. But even if I want to explore all of that, I know I won't. Not with her, not with anyone. I'm as explosive as the bomb that took my friends, my leg. I'm one tic away from detonating and destroying everything in my path.

I grab a hold of the counter and lift myself up off of the floor. I can't change Isabelle's looks. I can't stop my cock from begging for her. I can't even stop the hurricane of negativity that swirls around me.

What I *can* do is prepare for my mother's arrival. I can do that. I can buy furniture and turn my house into something that will ease her mind. And with that thought, I hop my way to the shower, unable to put any weight on my prosthesis because of the pain. When I reach the bathroom and sit on the edge of the tub, another thought occurs to me.

Almost as if I have no control over my movements, I lift my cell and punch a few keys. I hit send and hear the swoosh that tells me that it's too late to take back the text.

So much for focusing only on my mother and buying furniture.

# 11

# ISABELLE

*I* rub my temples to ease the headache that's developed to match the throbbing in my side where Doc stitched me up. My father begged me to take the day off, rest and let the healing process start, but I can't. My one-on-one sessions start next week with clients and I need to be prepared. Besides, if these veterans can get knocked down like they do and still get back up, so can I.

My phone vibrates across the wooden desk in my office. Wounded Warrior counselors are encouraged to work from home when they can, but I chose not to today. There's zero chance I would have been able to focus with everyone's hovering.

I wince at the pain when I reach for my cell, wishing I would have taken Doc up on his offer of pain meds. I'll have to rectify that when I get home but for now, ibuprofen is going to have to do. My eyes widen when I read the text from Finn.

**Are you busy? I could use your help.**

I flip the phone over and set it back down, telling myself that I'm not ignoring him but rather trying to prioritize work. I refocus my attention on the file of a Navy vet who was captured by insurgents and held as a POW for six months before being released. I make a mental note to talk to Brie. She's a kidnapping and torture survivor so she may be able to give me some insight as to the client's mental state.

The words on the papers begin to blur and my stomach rumbles, reminding me that I haven't eaten since before leaving my house this morning. I straighten the files on my desk and as I stand up, my phone vibrates again. I pick it up and read the text.

**Please...**

One thing I've learned about Finn is that 'please' isn't a normal part of his vocabulary so when he uses it, I find it's harder to ignore his request. I quickly respond, letting him know that I'll be done working around three and I'll swing by his place on my way home. He doesn't respond other than to react to my text with a thumbs up emoji and I can't stop the roll of my eyes at that.

I make my way out of my office, down the hallway toward the vending machines. I get a bag of chips and another of M&Ms. It's not much, but it'll get me through the next few hours. As I walk back to my office, my attention is drawn toward the receptionist's desk by a commotion.

"Miss Isabelle!"

I stifle the sigh that threatens at seeing Shane waving his arms at me. I can't exactly ignore him because he's a client, so I nod at the receptionist to allow him past.

"Told you she'd want to see me," I hear Shane say as he rounds the desk and closes the distance between us.

"What can I do for you, Shane?" I ask when he reaches me.

He glances at the snack food in my hands and his smile falters. "Oh, am I interrupting your lunch?"

"No, no," I assure him. I turn back toward my office and start walking. "Follow me. We can talk in my office."

"Okay."

I wait for him to cross the threshold before closing the door and returning to my chair. I set my food to the side and rest my hands on my desk. Shane sits in one of the two seats across from me.

"So, what brings you here, Shane?" I ask.

"Well, I wanted to make sure you were okay after last night. I didn't want to leave you alone with Finn, but Mama was waiting." His recollection of our interaction in the parking lot after group is a far cry from reality but I chalk it up to his brain injury. "She doesn't like to be kept…"

I listen to him go on and on about his 'Mama' and all the things he does to 'keep her happy'. Most of the words go in one ear and out the other because sitting up is uncomfortable at best and the ache is draining all of my attention.

In an effort to ease it, I lean back in my chair and try like hell to mask any discomfort I'm feeling. Apparently, I'm unsuccessful.

Shane's mouth shuts and he leans forward quickly, his eyes narrowing as he does. "What's wrong?" His concern is a startling contrast to the happy-go-lucky attitude he displayed a few seconds earlier.

I wave away his question. "Nothing. Rough workout," I lie.

He points toward my abdomen, his face reddening as the seconds pass. "Then why are you bleeding?"

I drop my gaze to see what he's talking about and dammit if he isn't right. Blood has soaked through my shirt and now that I'm paying attention, I can feel it trickling down my side as well. I yank open my desk drawer and grab a few tissues. As I press them to my side, I see a shadow fall over me.

"Here, let me."

It's Shane standing next to me but all I can think about is how Finn sounded when he said the same words to me last night after I got shot. It's Finn's hands I imagine coming closer, touching me, trying to help.

"What are you doing?" I snap when clumsy fingers try to lift my shirt.

Shane backs up quickly, hands up. "Nothing, Miss Isabelle. I... I want to help."

I inhale deeply, trying to center myself before I say something I can't take back. Shane is a client and, for reasons outside of his control, isn't all there. I'm supposed to be supportive of him, not disgusted or annoyed or pissed that he's not Finn.

"Sorry," I say, genuinely frustrated with my reaction to him.

Again, his demeanor shifts, so quickly I almost miss it before he pastes a smile back on his face. "It's okay." He shoves his hands in his pockets. "What happened?"

I try to come up with a lie that's believable, but I've got nothing. I can't tell him the truth, so I opt for changing the subject.

"So, you wanted to make sure I was okay after you left last night?"

He stares at me for a moment, his head tilted to the side. He seems to be deep in thought but shakes it off and replies. "Yes."

"Were you concerned about me being alone with Finn?" I ask, trying to determine the reasoning behind his curiosity so it can be addressed. That is my job, after all.

"He lied to you." He backs away from me and makes his

way toward the door. "He lies to everyone." He twists the doorknob and pushes it open. He glances over his shoulder one last time and says, "Mama's waiting. I have to go."

With that, he disappears so quickly I almost start to wonder if I imagined the entire interaction.

*Almost.*

I shake off the weird vibes that Shane left behind and grab the bag of M&Ms and my purse. I carry them with me, popping several candies into my mouth at a time, as I walk to the bathroom to clean my wound and redress it.

When I get back to my office with a fresh bandage in place and no M&Ms left, I lift the jacket I wore off of the back of my chair and put it on. There wasn't anything I could do about the blood stain on my shirt, and I don't want anyone else to see it and ask questions.

I spend the rest of the afternoon continuing to prep for my one-on-one sessions, paying extra attention to Shane's file. I want to help him but in order to do that, I need to understand him.

I lose track of time and the next thing I know, my phone is vibrating with a text. I rub my eyes and pick it up, seeing it's from Finn.

**Change your mind?**

I shift my eyes to look at the time and see that it's almost five. Shit!

**Sorry. Lost track of time. Be there in 15.**

Once I confirm that my response went through, I straighten the paperwork on my desk. I put Shane's file in my bag to take with me. I don't know that I'll gain any more insight into the man but if my instincts are right, there's something there. I just don't know what it is yet.

I shut the light off and pull the door closed, ensuring it's locked, before heading outside to my Harley. I push all thoughts of work from my mind and that's when everything else creeps in.

Thoughts of Finn. Thoughts of getting shot. Thoughts of Ann and her ex and his friends. When I pull into Finn's driveway, my mind is racing, questions are pulsating through my brainwaves and bunching up like a congested highway in rush hour traffic.

*Get your shit together, Iz.*

I push the kickstand down with my foot and dismount my bike. When I reach Finn's porch and lift my fist to knock, the door swings open and I'm met with over six feet of scowling man.

"Don't you ever fucking do that again!"

# 12

# FINN

"*W*hat the hell?"

I breathe deeply and try to get my racing heart under control. It took a lot for me to even ask Isabelle for her help. I told myself it wasn't because her opinion matters. I told myself that it wasn't because I wanted to see her. I lied to myself in so many ways… and then she was late. *Really* fucking late.

"Finn!" she snaps.

I realize I'm standing here like an idiot and blink several times to bring her face into focus. When I heard her Harley pull into the driveway, relief hit me hard. And then the rage took over and I reacted. How do I tell her that I was scared? How do I explain to her that I'm angrier with myself for letting my guard down when she said she'd come over after work?

"What?"

"What is your problem?"

I swallow every single emotion down and cross my arms over my chest. "You're late."

Isabelle tilts her head to the side and stares at me. "And I apologized for that," she reminds me. "I lost track of time."

I turn away from her, not trusting myself to say anything else. I hear Isabelle's footsteps on the floor, and I feel her gaze boring into my back. At least she's not burning a hole into my leg.

Her sigh is audible, and I have to make a conscious effort not to face her. "Look, I don't know why you're so angry. I was late, not standing you up."

"I know," I bark.

I grab my wallet off the counter and shove it in my back pocket. I turn and retrace my steps to the front door, not making eye contact when I pass her.

"Are you coming?" I ask, opening the door.

"Where are we going?" she asks, curiosity mingling with the frustration in her tone.

"You'll see."

Isabelle throws her hands up and shakes her head. "You're impossible."

She stomps back across the practically empty living room and out the front door. She doesn't slow until she reaches her Harley. I take my time locking the house up, knowing this next part isn't going to be easy... in any sense of the word.

When I reach my bike, I allow myself to look at her. "You're riding with me."

She narrows her eyes. "Why?"

*Because I can't get the image out of my mind of you laying in a ditch somewhere.*

"Does it matter?"

She huffs out a breath and makes her way toward my bike. "I guess not."

I straddle my Harley and wait for her to join me. When she settles behind me, it's all I can do not to flinch away from her. Not because I don't want her close but because I do. I want to feel her pressed against me. I want her arms

79

wrapped around me, her fingers linked to keep her in place. I *need* to feel her body heat, her heartbeat... *her*.

Her tits press against my back as she leans close, and my lungs seize.

"Are we gonna sit here all day?" Her breath rushes over my ear and my cock stirs.

I fire up my bike but it's another minute or two before I trust myself to even take off. When I do, she lurches backward, but only for a split second. She holds on tight, and I finally give in and let myself savor it.

I weave through traffic and try to keep my attention on the road but it's difficult. Hell, it's damn near impossible with Isabelle so close. When we're about a mile from our destination, I realize that I don't want the ride to end. I don't want her to pull away from me, even if it is just to get off the bike. So I take a left at the next light when I should be taking a right and head back in the direction of more rural roads.

Isabelle's hold on me loosens as the distance between us and traffic increases. It's clear she's comfortable on a Harley, whether she's the driver or the passenger. Not that I thought she wouldn't be, but it's one thing to instinctively know something and another entirely to experience it.

I don't allow the detour to last long. I have things that I need to do and realize I have no idea what time the store closes. I'm also not sure how much longer I can endure her body against mine. I love everything about it and that's a problem.

I point the bike back in the direction of my original destination. Another twenty minutes and I'm pulling into the parking lot at the furniture store. I find a space that's away from other vehicles. I never park close to anyone if I can help it. No point in inviting dings or issues with my Harley.

Isabelle swings her leg over the seat and steps away from

the Harley, away from me. Immediately, I miss her. I watch as her gaze shifts from me to the store front and back again.

"What are we doing here?"

"My mom is coming," I spit out, suddenly feeling stupid for asking for Isabelle's help.

Her eyes widen and her mouth falls open. She glances down at herself, as if to see if she looks okay. "What the hell, Finn? I can't meet your mother like this!"

"What? No." I take a step toward her. "She's not coming *here*. She's coming to visit next week."

Her mouth closes. "Oh." Again, she looks toward the store and then back to me. I can see the moment it hits her what we're doing here. "Wait. You want my help with picking out stuff for your house?"

"So?" I snap.

"It's just..." She braces her hands on her hips and shakes her head. "Why?"

I shrug like it's no big deal. "Because I don't know what the hell I'm doing." It's true, to a degree.

"You don't know how to pick out furniture and swipe your credit card when you're done?"

The grin on her face tells me she's teasing, as does the tone of her voice. And apparently, it's just what I need to lighten the mood. I chuckle, more at myself than her.

"Of course I can do that." I try to come up with a way to explain why I want her here without sounding like a complete idiot. "If you knew my mom, this would be so much easier for you to understand. She wants to know that I'm okay." I glance down at my leg and notice that I'm subconsciously rubbing my thigh. "She's worried about me." I take a deep breath. "And I may have told her that I'm fine and have moved past... well, this." I point to my leg.

Isabelle's face softens. "Oh. Well, then, we should go inside and see what kinda trouble we can get into."

She grabs my hand and starts dragging me toward the entrance. I could dig in my feet and refuse to budge but I don't. This is what I wanted. What I needed. Isabelle to come and make it all seem normal, somehow okay.

When we step through the door, she stops and faces me. "What kind of stuff do you like?"

"I don't know. Comfortable?"

"Are you asking me or telling me?" She laughs.

"Both."

Again, she shakes her head at me, all while she unzips her jacket and shrugs out of it. I don't bother to hide my appreciation of her body as she does this. My gaze travels from her face, down her neck to her shoulders, and then lower until it lands on—

"What the fuck is that?" I growl as I grab her arm and lift it slightly so I can see more of the red seeping through her shirt.

She looks down and her face pales. "Shit," she mumbles before returning her gaze to me. "I must have pulled my stitches again."

"Again?" I practically drag her back outside to avoid the stares that we were starting to garner. "When did you pull them the first time? Is that why you were late? What the hell happened?"

She holds her hand up to stop my rapid-fire questions. "Finn, calm down."

"Fuck that!" I shout and then slam my mouth shut as a couple walks past us with inquisitive looks on their faces. "Izzy, tell me what happened. Now!"

"Screw you," she snaps at me and yanks her arm out of my grasp. "You're not my keeper. You don't get to demand information from me. That's not how things work."

She's right. And I hate that she's right. But that doesn't stop the growing concern I'm feeling.

"Tell. Me. What. Happened."

Isabelle blows out a breath and her shoulders slump. "It's nothing. Really. My stitches pulled earlier at work and it started bleeding." She looks down at her blood-soaked shirt. "Doc can fix them when I get home."

Something about her explanation doesn't ring true. I narrow my eyes at her and lean close. "Why was that so hard to tell me?"

She averts her eyes for a moment before refocusing on me. "Can we go inside and get this over with? Please?"

"Sure." I shrug. "When you tell me the part of the story you're leaving out."

I take a step away from her and cross my arms over my chest. I can wait her out if I have to.

Isabelle rubs a hand over her forehead, seemingly thinking about what to say. "Shane stopped by my office today," she finally says.

My body tenses and an ache settles into my muscles. "And?"

"And nothing." She pins me with her gaze. "It was weird, is all."

I stare at her for a few more moments, wondering if she's going to give me more details or if she's going to leave it at that. When she remains silent, I decide to let it go. For now.

"Let's go inside and pick out some furniture."

Without thinking, I grab her hand and tug her along beside me. At first, she's stiff, resistant. But then she relaxes and links her fingers with mine. It feels... nice.

"You did see that the store closes in twenty minutes, right?" she asks, hitching a thumb over her shoulder to indicate the sign on the door.

"Yeah."

"Do you think you can pick out a couch that fast? And whatever else you need for your living room?"

I throw my head back and laugh. When I see the confusion on her face, I laugh harder.

"What's so funny?" She frowns.

"You are." When she continues to stare at me like I've lost my mind, I clarify. "Izzy, I need to furnish my whole fucking house, not just one room."

# 13

## ISABELLE

"*R*ough day?"

I should have known that Isaiah would track me down at Dusty's. When I'd left Finn's house, after promising to return tomorrow to help when his purchases are delivered, I'd come straight here. I needed a drink and to be alone.

"Something like that," I respond before downing the rest of my beer.

Ruby slides a beer across the bar for Isaiah and then disappears to handle other customers. My brother and I sit here, sipping our drinks and remaining silent. As soon as his bottle is empty, my reprieve ends.

"You need to have Doc take a look at your stitches."

I whip my head up and lock eyes with him. How did he—

"Finn called you?"

"Sure did," Isaiah replies with censure in his tone. "Care to tell me why he's the one telling me about shit you're dealing with and not you?"

"Not particularly," I snap.

Isaiah waves Ruby away when she tries to give him another beer. "Iz, what's going on?"

"Exactly what I told Finn… nothing."

"He didn't buy that and neither do I."

"Ruby, can I get a shot of tequila?" I call out over the music, avoiding Isaiah.

Only after I've downed the shot do I turn and face my brother.

"What exactly did Finn tell you?"

"That you pulled your stitches to the point that you were bleeding like a stuck pig." I roll my eyes at him when he pauses. "And that you have a stalker."

"You've gotta be fucking kidding me!"

Isaiah shakes his head. "Nope."

"I don't have a stalker," I insist. "I have a *client* who's weird. Nothing more."

"Why does Finn think this client is a stalker?"

"Ask Finn," I huff out.

"That's the thing… I did ask Finn. And he said that this Shane guy is a creep who has appointed himself as your savior. Finn says that Shane is someone we need to keep an eye on and that he's more dangerous because he seems so harmless."

That exact thought had already occurred to me. Shane is a creep who leaves me feeling like I've got a million spiders crawling all over my body. But that doesn't make him a bad person. And I'm certainly not afraid of him, nor would I call him a stalker.

"Finn's wrong."

"Yeah, see, I don't think he is," Isaiah retorts. "And I think that's exactly the reason why I had to hear it from him and not you."

"Isaiah, what do you want from me? I can't quit my job because Finn has a stupid feeling."

"No one is asking you to."

"Then what exactly are you asking? Because that isn't clear."

"Iz, I'm asking you to be careful. To not discount Finn's concerns because you're stubborn. I'm *asking* you to keep me in the loop."

"Fine."

"Thank you."

"Mmmm."

The music dies down, and I pick up my cell off the bar to check the time. It's almost eleven and I'm tired. I need to get back to the BRB so Doc can look at my stitches. I also need to get some sleep. Something tells me that tomorrow is going to be a long day.

∿

"Come on in."

Finn steps to the side to let me in. I'm careful not to brush against him as I pass and make my way to his kitchen. I set down the cups of coffee I brought with me, along with the box of donuts. When I turn around to face the living room, I bump into a wall of muscle.

Finn's hands settle on my shoulders. "Whoa." He stoops down to look me in the eye. "Are you okay?"

*No, I'm not okay. I'm sleep deprived, sex deprived, and don't want to be here.*

"Uh huh."

Finn raises a brow but drops his arms. "You brought coffee?" He nods toward the items I set down.

"And donuts. I brought donuts too."

"I see that." He glances at the box. "A lot of donuts."

I turn to grab a cream-filled eclair and take a bite. A blob of cream seeps from the end of the sweet goodness and I stick my tongue out to lick it off. Finn's eyes never leave my mouth as I do. I finish the donut without a word and when I reach for another, Finn's hand settles on my arm.

I glance at it and then back to him. His lips are pulled into a frown, like he's confused about what is happening. And I get it because I know I sure as hell don't have a clue about the electrical charge in the air.

"How's your side?" He nods toward my abdomen.

I swallow the bite of donut in my mouth and lick my lips before answering. "Good. Doc put new stitches in." I shrug as if it didn't hurt like the devil. "Told me to be careful not to pull them again."

"I probably shouldn't have asked you to come help today," he mumbles.

"Lucky for you, I thought ahead."

As if on cue, there's a knock on his door. He narrows his eyes, and a rumble comes from him.

"Who the fuck is that?" he snarls as he turns to walk to the door.

"Reinforcements," I say cheerily.

Finn yanks the door open and comes face to face with Isaiah, Liam, and Cooper.

"I take it you didn't know we were coming," Isaiah says around a chuckle. He steps around Finn, clapping him on the back as he does, and then pins me with a stare. "Iz, I told you to tell him."

"I was just getting—"

"I was promised food," Liam says as he walks around Finn. His eyes light up when they land on the box of pastries. "Ah, there they are."

Before Cooper can walk around him, Finn steps to the side to let him in. Finn's face is a mask of confusion and frustration and for a moment, I wonder if I did something wrong is asking the guys to help.

"You might as well get used to it, brother," Cooper says. "Trust me, the sooner you accept the fact that you're one of us, the better. Because if there's one thing I've learned since meeting these yahoos, it's that once they claim you there's no going back to life without them."

Color creeps into Finn's cheeks and I can't tell if it's from anger or embarrassment, but I think it's the former. He doesn't strike me as the type to get embarrassed by much of anything and he's proven that he's quick to anger.

I ignore the three stooges and close the distance between Finn and me.

"I'm sorry, Finn."

I reach out to touch his arm, fully expecting him to flinch away, and pleasantly surprised when he doesn't.

"I can make them leave if you want."

Finn's eyes narrow and he glares at me. "Do you really think I can't handle some furniture?"

Shocked by his words, I rear back as if slapped. I drop my arm to my side and swallow past a growing lump in my throat.

"What? Why would you think that?"

"All you see when you look at me is a fucking cripple! So much so that you needed to ask *real* men to help."

"That's not—"

"I've got news for you," he snarls as if I wasn't speaking. "I'm not a goddamn cripple!"

"I know that," I cry, desperate for him to calm down. "I've never once thought you were." My own anger springs to life inside of me, sparking the embers of my temper. "I asked them to help because I knew I wouldn't be able to do much with my gunshot wound. Remember that? The fact that I was shot the other day?"

"Of course I remember," he barks. "I was there when it happened." Finn storms away from me, toward the kitchen.

"Let's not pretend that's why they're here." He jabs a finger in the air to indicate my brother, Liam, and Cooper.

"Finn," Isaiah starts. "You need to calm down." Finn says nothing so Isaiah keeps talking. "You're the only one here who thinks of yourself as a cripple. No one—and certainly not Iz—sees you as anything but a man with a serious fucking attitude."

"Look, if you want us to leave, all you gotta do is ask," Liam says. "We're only trying to help but if you'd rather do it all by yourself, fine."

Isaiah steps closer to Finn, barely leaving any room between them. "But know this… If you think for one second that you can talk to Iz that way and get away with it, you're sadly mistaken." Isaiah looks at me and grins. "I know she doesn't need me to fight her battles, but I don't care. She's done nothing wrong, and I'll be damned if I sit by and watch you tear into her because of your own demons. She deserves better than that."

Isaiah signals to Liam and Cooper that it's time to leave and I watch them walk to the door, too stunned to say anything.

"Wait," Finn calls before they step through the threshold. All three of them look back to him. "Don't leave."

"What's that?" Isaiah asks. "I didn't quite hear you."

Isaiah's just being a dick now, making Finn suffer a bit.

"I'm sorry," Finn pushes out.

"Don't apologize to us," Liam says and nods toward me. "We're not the ones you need forgiveness from."

I roll my eyes. I appreciate what they're doing but I don't need their help. The problem is, I've learned when to let them do their thing and when to argue. This is not the time to argue.

Finn pins me with his eyes, his face still red and his shoulders tense. "Izzy, I'm—"

"Furniture delivery is here," Cooper informs the room, seemingly not caring that Finn was trying to talk. "We'll help unload the truck while you two talk. Finn, take her to your bedroom or something to have your conversation."

My eyes widen at the suggestion that we go to the bedroom, as do Finn's, but he heads toward another room. Isaiah shakes his head and chuckles, although I fail to see what's so funny.

I follow Finn's path and enter his bedroom, or at least I assume it's his bedroom because it's where he went. The lack of furniture makes it hard to determine otherwise.

"Finn—"

"Iz—"

I close my mouth to let him go first. He closes the door and leans his forehead against it, his back to me. Several long moments pass in silence and I begin to wonder if he's going to say anything at all. When he straightens, he doesn't turn around, but he does speak.

"You make me crazy."

Unsure what he means, I wait to see if he's going to explain. He doesn't leave me wondering long before he whirls around, and I see the frustration etched into the lines of his face.

"When I'm around you, I can't think straight. I don't know how to act around you because one day you're my counselor, the next you're a member of the BRB, and the next you're a woman I want to fuck senseless and push away at the same time."

His admission stuns me, so much so that I have no idea how to respond.

"Isaiah's right... you deserve so much better." He takes a step toward me. "But God help me, the thought of you finding *better* with someone else makes me insane. And I have no idea what to do with that."

I swallow, trying to gather my thoughts. "Finn, I—"

"I'm not done," he snaps, cutting me off. "I want you, Iz. I have since the moment I first saw your face, after you almost ran me over." I open my mouth to speak, and he holds his hand up to stop me. "Still not done." Finn takes a deep breath. "I have no fucking clue how to be around you and not want you. Sure, you frustrate the hell out of me, but I like that. I like that you don't take my shit. I like that you're strong and independent and smart and beautiful." He reaches out and tucks a strand of hair behind my ear. "I don't know how to handle that. I'm not the man I was before the bombing. I can't be the man you need, the man you deserve. I'm broken, damaged beyond repair, and I know it." He shrugs. "So I push you away. I rage at you, find fault in everything you do. Because it makes it easier to keep you at arm's length. It makes it easier for me to not act on every single thought and feeling and *craving*."

I can't make sense of what he's saying so I focus on the one bit of information that keeps getting snagged on the tentacles of my mind. "Do you seriously believe that your damn leg makes you less of a man?"

His face hardens and he nods.

"You're a fucking idiot!" I shout, shoving against his chest, and his eyes widen. "I don't care about your leg. I'm not that shallow and it pisses me off that you think I am."

"I don't think you're shallow," he insists.

"Yeah, Finn, you do." I tilt my head. "Do you want to know what I see when I look at you?" I don't give him a chance to answer. "I see a man who has given up, a man who has let his trauma define him. I see a man who doesn't see himself at all. You should have the world by the balls but instead you're rolling over in defeat." I shake my head. "When we first met, you said that I couldn't hack it, that I wouldn't understand anything that the vets have gone through. Well,

I've got news for you," I poke his chest with a finger. "You're the one who can't hack it. You're the one who has no idea how to handle your trauma."

"Izzy," he growls, warning clear in those two syllables.

"What?" I throw my arms up. "Go ahead, Finn, tear into me. I can take it." I take a deep breath, blow it out slowly. "The question is, can you?"

Finn runs shaky hands through his hair, clearly rattled. Good, he should be. He's pushed me too far this time.

"The sad thing about this is, I thought we'd made progress yesterday. I thought you were finally starting to see me for who I am and not some inconvenient person who'll get in the way of your pity party. But you don't see me at all."

I push past him and storm out into the living room, toward the front door. I ignore the worried glances of my brothers, both blood and club. When I reach the driveway, I straddle my Harley and fire it up. The delivery truck is blocking my exit, but I don't let that stop me. I go through the yard, not giving a damn if it creates ruts and get the hell out of there.

Fuck Finn.

Fuck him and his issues.

Fuck all of it.

## 14

---

## FINN

"*What* the hell?"

I can't bring myself to look at Isaiah. No doubt he heard some of Isabelle's outburst and he couldn't have missed her leaving like she did. I walk to the kitchen and pull a beer out of the fridge. I twist the top off and toss it on the counter.

"Little early to be drinking, don't you think?" Liam asks from his position at the front door.

"It's five o'clock somewhere," I mumble after I kill off the brew and toss the empty bottle in the trash.

"Yeah, but not here," Cooper joins in. "Dude, I told you to apologize, not send her running."

"Someone should probably go after her," I say, ignoring their concerns.

"And that someone should be you," Isaiah prods.

I look at the furniture that's now cluttering my living room, taking up every free inch. "I need to deal with—"

"We've got this," Isaiah assures me. "I think we can figure out what room everything goes in. And if we get it wrong, you can move it." I raise my brow at him. "What? I don't care

94

about your fucking prosthetic. Bum leg or not, you can handle it."

I heave a sigh. It seems Isabelle was right... I'm the only one who thinks my leg is an issue. "Any ideas where she might be headed?"

"Elephant Hill."

"Where?"

"It's a place we all like to go when we need to be alone." Isaiah spends the next few minutes giving me directions. "If she's not there, try her office. She won't go home. Too much chance someone will drop in."

"Thanks, man."

"You're welcome." He slaps me on the back. "But if you send her running again, I can't be held responsible for my actions."

I chuckle, finally feeling some of my tension ease. "Got it."

"He's not joking," Cooper says. "And even if he were, the rest of us would handle it for him."

"Right." I step through the front door and glance over my shoulder. "Thank you. Seriously. I know I don't deserve your help, but it's appreciated."

"Don't mention it. We're family and this is what family does."

I nod and make my way to my bike. The delivery truck is gone so I pull out of the driveway as fast as I can. I go in the direction Isaiah told me to go, toward Elephant Hill. It takes me thirty minutes to get there so I use the time to think about what to say to Isabelle when I see her.

Her bike is parked by the side of the road and I pull behind it, shutting mine off. I sit there for a few minutes and watch her at the top of the hill. The wind whips her hair and there's something sad about it.

When I feel relatively confident that I won't put my foot

in my mouth again, I walk up the hill, ignoring the way my prosthesis chafes. My pain isn't important right now.

"How'd you get him to tell you where I'd be?" she asks when I'm within earshot.

"Paid him a thousand bucks."

Her eyes widen. "Seriously?"

I shake my head. "No." I smile, something I realize I don't do often enough around her. "But I would have."

"Why?" she asks, guarded.

"Because…"

"That's not an answer," she complains.

"I know." I sit down next to her, the action awkward with my prosthetic. "I meant it when I said you make me crazy." I bump her shoulder in an effort to relieve some of the tension between us, but it doesn't work. I heave a sigh. "Izzy, I'm sorry."

"For?"

"Everything."

"That's a copout for people who apologize with no idea what they actually did wrong."

"Maybe, but not in this case. I know I fucked up. I know that I said things I shouldn't have, and I hurt you. And for that, I'm sorry."

She nods and then tips her head back to stare at the sky. My eyes are drawn to the slender column of her neck, the way her throat works when she swallows. My dick twitches so I shift to adjust myself.

"Do you want to know what I see when I look at you?" she asks.

"You made it pretty clear back at my place that you don't see anything good," I remind her, not wanting to hear it all again.

She shifts so she's facing me. "I'm sorry about that."

"Don't be. You were just being honest."

"No, I wasn't," she says quietly. "I was lashing out because you pissed me off."

"Okay," I concede. "Then what do you see?"

"I see everything." Her statement is so matter of fact, I feel like I'm missing something, but she quickly continues. "I see a man who thinks so little of himself that he's forgotten all the good. You're a good man, Finn." She reaches out and rests her hand on my knee. "Sure, you've got scars, both physical and emotional, but that doesn't make you less than who you were before you got them." She breathes deeply and averts her eyes, but she doesn't remove her hand. "I look at you and I see my past, present, and future all rolled into one perfectly imperfect human." She returns her gaze to my face. "I see you, Finn. All of you."

"But—"

She holds a hand up. "I'm not done. I don't know if there's something between us or if we're just two people who happen to be lonely. I don't know if it's even worth exploring. What I do know, is this." She pauses for a second and then a smile lights up her face. "I know that you bring out the best and the worst in me. I know that you're the kind of man who will be my equal and not shrink under the weight of the club. I know that, despite your rough exterior, you're a softy on the inside, in the best possible way."

"I'm not a softy," I grumble.

Isabelle cocks her head to the side. "Finn, you went out and bought furniture just to make your mom happy." She laughs. "It would have been so much easier for you to wallow and sulk and toss your mom to the side because you're caught up in your own shit. But you didn't. You did everything in your power to make sure she believes you're okay. Not to mention, the bullshit pep talks you give at group."

"No point in dragging everyone else down with me."

"See," she exclaims. "That's what I'm talking about. As

much as you try and hide away, as much as you say that you're worthless or not good enough... you don't truly believe it. If you did, you'd never leave your house."

Isabelle's words begin to penetrate the fog that has clouded my every waking moment for almost two years. I think back over all of my speeches to other veterans, all my conversations with my mother, all of the negativity that I've held on to for so long. Isabelle is right. It would have been a lot easier if I hadn't tried so hard to keep up appearances. And that makes me wonder why I did try so hard.

*Because you're not a quitter.*

I want to promise her that I'll never push her away again. I want to ask her to give me a chance, to stick out my sour moods and angry outbursts. But I have no right to ask that of her. But there is something I can do that's a step in the right direction.

I reach into my back pocket to grab my wallet and pull out three one-hundred-dollar bills. I thrust them in her direction, and she only stares at my outstretched hand.

"What's that for?"

"It should be a thousand, but this is all I've got." I shake the bills at her until she takes them, confusion still etched in her expression. "I bet you a thousand bucks that you couldn't hack it," I remind her. "I was wrong."

Isabelle throws her head back and laughs, the sound settling in my bones and making me feel lighter than I have in a very long time.

# 15

# ISABELLE

"*T*ell me, tell me, tell me."

I don't even bother hiding my grin at Tillie. It's been two days since Finn and I had it out and honestly, I'm surprised it took Tillie this long to come looking for information.

"Not sure I can tell you more than Isaiah already has," I say, laughing.

"Bullshit. All I got out of him was that you and Finn had a fight, you stormed out and Finn went after you.'

"That about sums it up."

"I repeat, bullshit!"

I open my mouth to speak just as Ruby steps up to the bar. "I want details, too. Liam was no help."

"You two are horrible," I joke.

What I don't say is that I've missed this. I've missed being able to 'gossip' with friends, to laugh about guys, to just be a girl.

"Girl, you better start dishing or—"

"I wanna know, too."

I whirl around and see Lila standing behind my barstool. I raise a brow at her.

"What?" she asks.

Tillie swats my arm. "I texted her and told her to get here if she wanted the scoop." She hands out the shots that the bartender set on the bar. "Now, tell us what the hell happened with Finn and what's going on with the two of you. Your brother seems to think you two are an item and I need to know if he's right."

I down the shot of tequila and slam the empty glass on the bar top. "We aren't an item," I finally say.

"But you want to be?" Ruby asks, apparently hearing the disappointment in my tone that I couldn't hide.

"I don't know." I lift my hand for the bartender to get us another round. Ruby could get them but it's her night off and we all try hard not to take advantage of her when she's not actually working. "I mean, I like him. And I'm pretty sure the feeling is mutual."

"So what's the problem?" Lila asks.

"There isn't one," I say, not entirely sure that's the truth. "We're just not putting a label on anything right now."

"Has he asked you out on a date?" Tillie pipes up.

"I don't know if it's a date but we're taking a ride tomorrow."

Tillie groans, seemingly not satisfied with my answers. "Are you taking one Harley or two?"

"One... I think."

"Then it's a date."

Before I have a chance to contemplate that, my phone buzzes in my back pocket and I pull it out. It's a text from a number I don't recognize so I lay it on the bar, ignoring it.

"Any idea what you'll wear?" Lila asks.

"Jeans?"

"Jesus, Iz, you have to put *some* thought into it," Ruby

groans. When we stare at her like she's been inhabited by an alien, she throws her hands up. "What? I know I'm not the most girly girl, but I do know some things."

My cell buzzes again, causing it to slide around on the bar top.

"Is that him?" Tillie asks and reaches for the phone before I can stop her. "I'm gonna tell him to…"

Her words trail off and her face scrunches up. She taps the screen a few times and I watch as she scrolls, thinking she's reading old texts from Finn, not that there are many.

"Iz, you've got a problem," she says, her tone serious.

She turns the phone so I can see the texts and my stomach bottoms out when I see how many there are. The most recent one draws my attention and it's all I can do not to grab the phone from Tillie and smash it to pieces.

**You're putting your friends in danger.**

I stand up and turn around to survey the bar. It's a weekday so it's not crowded, and no one looks suspicious or unfamiliar. Ruby and Lila rush outside, presumably to check the parking lot, and when they return, both are shaking their heads.

I pull up the text messages again and skim through them. A few jump out at me.

**I could have killed you. Next time, I won't be so nice.**

**You shouldn't trust your life to a cripple.**

**Maybe you should rethink your job… again.**

**Really, Isabelle? Out in the open, on a hill? You make this too easy.**

The more I read, the more my skin crawls. How long has he been watching me? *Who* is watching me?

"Isaiah's on his way," Tillie says. I turn toward Tillie and nod. "I asked him to bring Finn."

Knowing Finn will be here soon gives me the comfort I didn't even realize I needed. "Okay."

"Iz, who are these texts from?"

"I don't know."

"Have you had any issues or run-ins with anyone at work? A client? Coworker? Any new BRB clients?"

"No, no one that I…" I shake my head. "Shane," I say with a sigh.

"Who?"

"He's a client. Finn's been trying to get me to see that he's a problem but, I don't know." I struggle to come up with the words. "It just doesn't feel right that it would be him. He's weird and creepy but this?" I lift my phone. "This goes way beyond weird and creepy."

"He's worth looking into though, right? If Finn is concerned, he's gotta have a reason."

"I've got Shane's file at home." When Tillie's eyes narrow, I give a self-deprecating smile. "I'd already decided to do some digging. I don't think this is him but I'm also not stupid."

"You think it's Ann's ex, don't you?" Tillie asks. She knows me so well.

"That's the only thing that makes sense." I look back at the texts. "But I don't know. This feels… different."

Ruby and Lila join us back at the bar. "Liam and Cooper are on their way."

"Damn," I mutter, earning myself a few glares. "Do we really need all of them?"

Lila shrugs. "Probably not but when there's a problem, we want them here. Not because we can't take care of ourselves but because they love us." She rests a hand on my shoulder. "It's called family, Iz. That's what you do with family, with people you love. You call them."

"Sorry." I sigh. "I'm not trying to be a bitch."

"You're scared."

"No, I'm not," I rush to refute them. "I'm annoyed. There's a difference."

Tillie, Ruby and Lila continue to talk about their significant others and what they all think should be our focus. I tune them out and stare at my phone. This is ridiculous. I open the messaging app and punch out a quick text.

**Who is this?**

I don't expect a response but—
My phone dings and I'm surprised.

**Who do you think it is?**

*If I knew, I wouldn't have asked, asshole.*
Before I have a chance to respond, another text comes through.

**It doesn't matter who I am. All that matters is you take me seriously.**

A commotion at the door draws my attention and I turn in time to see Isaiah, Liam, and Cooper shoving through. Finn is right behind them but as soon as he clears the threshold, he picks up his pace and is beside me in seconds.

"Are you okay?" he asks, sounding out of breath.

"Did you run here?" I ask, trying to lighten the mood.

"Izzy," he growls.

"I'm fine." I hand him my phone. "Just pissed off."

Finn reads through the texts and as he's skimming, the cell dings again.

Finn's eyes narrow as he reads the latest text out loud. "Wrong move, princess. Call off your dogs or else." His gaze shifts to check out our surroundings and when his shoulders slump, I know he's come to the same conclusion I did. There's no one out of place here.

Finn hands the phone to Isaiah and then he wraps an arm around my waist. Whether to comfort me or himself, I don't know, nor do I care. It feels good and if I'm being honest, it's exactly what I need to ground myself.

When Isaiah's done reading through the texts, he hands the cell to Liam. "See what you can get from this."

"Done," Liam assures him as he taps the screen several times, no doubt doing some tech thing I wouldn't understand. When he looks up, he grins. "Sent everything to my dad to get started."

"Thanks."

"No problem." Liam steps up to Ruby and wraps his arms around her from behind. "You okay?" he asks her.

"Of course," she responds. "But I'm better now."

She turns in his arms and fuses her mouth to his. Tillie does the same to Isaiah and Lila and Cooper start making out, too.

"Well," Finn begins, rocking back on his heels.

"Welcome to my world."

I try to force a laugh, but it doesn't come.

Finn locks eyes with me, his pupils dilating. "I like your world."

"Oh," I murmur as his face inches closer to mine.

His lips meet mine, tentatively, as if he's afraid to spook me. No chance of that happening. I wrap my arms around his neck, and he lifts me off my feet and settles me onto the bar top. He steps between my legs, never breaking the kiss.

My lips part and Finn's tongue dips into my mouth, tantalizing mine. He tastes like a heady mixture of desperation, need, and desire. It's an intoxicating mixture, one I find that matches my own swirling feelings.

I don't know who is texting me and at this moment, I couldn't care less. If this is what 'calling my dogs' gets me, I'll call them over and over and over again.

# 16

# FINN

*I* watch Isabelle from the doorway to her office. She's bent over a file on her desk, deep in thought, and making notes in the margins of the paper every few minutes. It's been less than twenty-four hours since I threw caution to the wind and kissed her and all I want is to do it again. But that's not why I'm here.

I clear my throat to get her attention and enjoy the way her lips part when she's startled. Her cheeks pinken and the way her gaze drops from my face, down to my groin, and back up again tells me she's remembering our kiss too.

"Is that how you greet all your clients?" I ask.

"What?" she snaps, clearly rattled. "No, of course not."

I push off the doorframe and sit in the chair across from her. "Good."

She pushes a strand of hair out of her face and leans back in her office chair. "What are you doing here, Finn?" She's trying to sound annoyed and failing miserably.

"I came to tell you what Liam found out about Shane." I toss the papers on her desk that I brought with me. "I wanted you to know before group."

Isabelle glances at the paper but makes no move to pick it up. "Just tell me. You were right, weren't you?" Ah, there's the annoyance I know and love.

*Love? When did you start thinking in terms of love?*

I debate on dragging this out for my benefit but decide against it. "Actually, no, I wasn't."

"What?" She grabs the papers and skims through them. "There's nothing here."

"Exactly," I confirm. "Liam couldn't find a damn thing that would link him to the texts or the shooting. He's creepy but it seems it really is because of his brain injury."

Isabelle's body seems to deflate, and she looks at me with despair. "Then who is it, Finn? What do they want?"

I lean forward and stretch my arm across the desk. When I open my hand, she places hers in it and I squeeze. It all feels foreign and somehow… natural.

"I don't know, Izzy."

The thing I have to remember about Isabelle is that, despite being strong and independent, she's still human. And sometimes a person needs reassurance whether they ask for it or not. Sometimes they just need to be reminded that they aren't alone and that they're safe.

With that in mind, I stand and scoot around the desk. I urge her up and pull her into my arms. She doesn't resist but rather settles into my chest and wraps her arms around my waist.

"Do you trust me?" I ask, resting my head on hers.

She nods.

"Then trust that I'm here and you don't have to figure this all out on your own." I urge her away from me so I can look her in the eyes. "I know you have your brother and your club, and maybe you don't need me too, but I'm here anyway."

"Why?"

"Because I want to be."

"Are you sure, Finn? Because I really like you and I don't think I can handle a love her and leave her type of thing on top of everything else."

"I'm sure."

"Okay."

She sits back down, and I return to my chair.

"Are you going to group with me? Even though it's not Shane?"

"Izzy, I went to group before you came into my life and I'm going to keep going. As much as I may act otherwise, it's good for me."

She nods. "Good."

"Besides, I'm not ruling Shane out completely." When she opens her mouth to protest, I push on. "I know what Liam found, or didn't find. I get that it's not likely it's Shane. But it's not worth the risk, just in case. Why take the chance?"

She seems to think about my words and then sighs heavily. "Agreed. But I don't like it. It feels wrong somehow to not trust my club."

"It has nothing to do with trust." When she looks skeptical, I clarify. "Izzy, it's about being smart and alert. I bet Liam is right about Shane. But if he's wrong, we'll be prepared. Not to mention, we still don't know who the fuck it is, if not Shane. It could be anyone. Until we know, we take no chances."

She chuckles. "You're gonna be bossy as hell through this, aren't you?"

"Eh, probably," I confirm. "But I'll try not to be."

"I'm not some helpless flower, ya know."

"I do know. Cut me some slack, okay. All my manly instincts tell me to protect you, your own capabilities and strong-will be damned."

Her chuckle turns into a full belly laugh. "I swear to God,

Finn, if you start beating on your chest like a damn caveman, we're going to have issues."

"No chest beating." And because I can't resist, I say, "At least not in any way that could be misconstrued as caveman-like."

I wink at her and she blushes. It's all I can do not to lunge across the desk and take her right here, right now, so I force my thoughts in a different direction.

"Not to keep circling back to it, but are there any other clients who stand out to you as potential suspects?"

Isabelle shakes her head. "Not really. I mean, I haven't been involved with any of them that long to know for sure, but I've gone through every file with a fine-tooth comb." She shrugs. "I didn't see anything."

"We should have Liam check into all of them, just to be sure."

"No, we shouldn't." She leans back in her chair. "Finn, I can't do that. Hell, I shouldn't have done that with Shane. It violates so many privacy laws and policies it's not even funny."

"I don't give a damn about privacy," I bite out. "I want you safe."

"And I *do* give a damn," she counters. "If someone does or says something that's concerning, I'll get Liam to start digging but for now, we let it rest. At least as far as my clients go."

I want to argue but I don't. She has a point, although I don't like it. "Fine."

Isabelle glances toward the clock on the wall and begins clearing her desk. "We should go," she says when she stands, her tone clipped.

An uneasy feeling settles over me. "Izzy, what's wrong?"

"I hate this," she snaps and shoves a hand through her blonde hair. "I feel like a sitting duck. Don't get me wrong,

I'm glad it's not Shane, or *not likely* Shane, but we're back at square one."

"I know. But we'll figure it out. In the meantime, we stay alert and cautious."

I throw my arm around her shoulders and we walk down the hall and outside.

"Wasn't it you who said I was reckless?" she asks.

I blow out a breath. "Yeah, I did say that. But that was more about me than it ever was about you."

"Miss Isabelle!"

Isabelle stiffens next to me and we both slowly turn around to see Shane running up behind us. When he's a few feet away, he glares at me and he clenches his fists at his sides.

"What are you doing with *him*?" Shane nods in my direction and thinly veiled rage drips from his words. "I told you he's a liar."

I take a threatening step forward and Isabelle wraps her hand in my shirt to hold me back. I glance at her and she shakes her head. I breathe deeply to regain some control and step aside to let Isabelle handle the situation.

"Shane, who I choose to spend my time with is none of your concern." Her tone is firm but polite and she's smiling sweetly. It's all I can do not to roll my eyes. "I appreciate that you want to look out for me but I'm fine. I can take care of myself."

"B-but..." Shane's eyes dart from her to me and back again. "He's not good enough for you!"

"I'll decide who is or isn't good enough for me."

Shane begins to tremble and when he tries to come closer to Isabelle, I put my arm up to stop him.

"Shane, don't," I snarl.

He bristles and struggles against my arm.

"Let go of me."

"That's not happening," I inform him.

"I... you..."

His mouth opens and closes several times before giving up. He whirls around and practically runs in the direction he came from. Isabelle and I exchange a look, concern and confusion warring for both of us.

"That was weird," she finally says.

"Very," I agree.

"Maybe Liam is wrong."

"Maybe."

Isabelle lifts her head to look me in the eyes. "Are you going to agree with everything I say or tell me what you're really thinking?"

I grin and shrug. "Both. Shane's behavior *is* weird, but we already knew that. And as for Liam being right or wrong, only time will tell."

She starts walking toward the building group is in, leaving me to trail behind her. Sensing that she needs time to herself to sort through her thoughts and process the last few minutes, I let her stay ahead of me. What I don't do is let her out of my sight.

One can never be too careful, and when it comes to Isabelle, I'll leave nothing to chance.

# 17

# ISABELLE

*J* watch as clients filter into the room, taking their seats in the circle. There are a few new faces, ones I recognize from their individual files and there are those who I've already met. I watch the time on my phone to ensure that I get things started on time and just as I stand, with a minute left, one last person strides through the door.

The fine hairs on the back of my neck stand up and I spare Finn a glance to see if he's noticed the newcomer. Based on the way he's risen from his chair and his shoulders are bunched, along with his narrow-eyed stare, he has.

"Oh, what? Not happy to see me?"

Finn explodes and storms toward Carson, Ann's ex-husband, arms outstretched to grab a hold of him the second he's within reach. Carson doesn't move a muscle. I lunge toward them both and manage to latch onto Finn's arm before he can connect with Carson.

"Finn, stop," I order without taking my eyes off of Carson. "He's not worth it."

"What are you doing here?" Finn demands.

Carson rocks back on his heels as if he doesn't have a care

in the world. "Just checking out the brick fucking wall that Ann's put between her and me." His grin is full of hatred. "I have to say, I'm not impressed."

Footsteps sound behind me and I look over my shoulder to see a client walking toward us.

"Everything okay here?" they ask.

"We're fine," I assure the man, doing my best to smile reassuringly. I take in all of my clients who have looks of concern on their faces. "Group is cancelled for the night," I call out.

"Smart move," Carson sneers. "No point in putting them in danger."

A chill races down my spine at his words.

*You're putting your friends in danger.*

The text from the other night flashes like a neon sign in my mind, grabbing hold of my senses and twisting.

"It was you."

Finn twists to glance at me, his brows pinched in question. I shove him away, no longer caring if I'm the only thing stopping him from beating the shit out of Carson. I step toward Carson and allow myself to feel the fear, the fury.

"You sent all those texts. You're the one who shot me!" I shout.

Carson rears back and raises his hands defensively. "Shot you? I didn't fucking shoot nobody."

I lift my shirt to expose the stitched-up wound. "You did this." He averts his gaze. "Look at it, asshole! Look at what you did."

Noise surrounds me as everyone shuffles out of the room. I can feel a few stares, lingering glances from curious clients. But no one says a word. No one asks any questions.

"Lady, you're nuts," Carson finally grumbles, still not looking at me.

My chest heaves as I try to suck in oxygen. Tension builds

in my veins and my pulse explodes in my ears. The space around me seems to shrink until all that's left is me, myself, and I. And Finn. I can't see him, he's not inside the black hole that my vision has diminished to, but I feel him, sense him.

I hear a muffled voice but can't make out the words. I strain, trying to determine who's talking, and that only makes the pulsating inside my body worse.

"Isabelle?"

*Finn?*

A light touch on my arm pulls me out of the mental sinkhole but I get caught up on something, something that keeps me rooted.

"Izzy!"

I'm yanked from the void and jarred into reality.

"He's gone."

"What?" I look around the room. "Why? Where did he go?"

"It wasn't him, Izzy."

My glare falls on Finn's face. "Yes it was! You heard him. He said almost exactly the same thing that was in that text."

"Yeah, I heard him." Finn rests his hands on my shoulders to hold me in place. "I also saw his reaction when you tried to get him to look at the gunshot wound. It wasn't him."

"You can't know that."

"It. Wasn't. Him."

"Yes it—"

"Isabelle!" Finn snaps. "He's an abusive asshole but he's not the shooter. It takes a certain kind of evil to pull the trigger when the target is a human. Trust me. I've seen it time and time again in the military. He couldn't even stand to look at a stitched-up bullet wound. One that isn't even all that gory. There's no way that he has the stomach to cause it."

The door crashes open, pulling my attention away from

Finn. When my eyes land on my brother, I can't stop myself from lashing out.

"You called Isaiah?" I demand of Finn. "Jesus, why?"

"He called me because our case has put you in danger." Isaiah reaches my side and seems to look me over. "Well, you don't look like you're hurt. Are you okay?"

"I'm fine," I groan. "Just rattled."

"Iz, don't lie to me."

The weight of the world seems to crash down around me, and my eyes burn with unshed tears.

"I would've bet my life that it was him."

Finn pulls me toward him, and I lean into his side. "And you had every reason to suspect him. No one faults you for that. But it wasn't—"

"Him," I finish dryly. "Yeah, you've said that already."

"Finn, are you one hundred percent certain it's not Carson who's targeting Iz?"

"A hundred percent?" Finn shakes his head. "No. I want Liam to dig into him again, just to be sure, but my gut says it's not him and I trust my gut."

"Good enough for me."

A thought takes form in my mind and I stiffen. "Ann." Her name comes out breathy. "Someone needs to check on Ann."

"Already on it. Liam and Cooper went straight to her house while I came here."

I nod, relieved that she wasn't forgotten. "Just because he's not the guy after me doesn't make him any less danger-ous. He showed up here, out of nowhere, and he was angry. I'm worried that he's escalating."

"We're not taking any chances with Ann, Iz," Isaiah assures me. "But as of today, Finn and I are making you *our* priority."

As little as an hour ago, I would have argued with my brother about that. I would have insisted that I can take care of myself, that I don't need their protection and hovering. Now? I'm not so sure.

"Thanks."

"I think you should stay with me," Finn suggests, and I whip my head in his direction. "What? It makes the most sense. I don't want you alone."

"It makes more sense for me to stay on the property. It's more secure." Finn opens his mouth to argue but I don't give him a chance. "I appreciate the offer, Finn. I really do. But I'm safer at home. Besides, your mom is flying into town tomorrow. You're going to be busy."

"Fuck!"

"You forgot, didn't you?"

Finn narrows his eyes. "No."

"Yeah, you did." I shake my head at him and chuckle. "I'm not judging. It's not like you've been sitting on your ass."

"Fine, I forgot." He takes a few deep breaths. "Maybe I should call her and reschedule."

"Don't do that," Isaiah says. "Family comes first. Always. We'll make sure Iz is safe."

"Why don't you bring her to the main house tomorrow evening for dinner?" I suggest.

"Are you sure?" Finn's gaze darts from me to Isaiah and back again. "I don't want to be a bother."

Isaiah slaps Finn on the back. "Family, brother. We'd love to meet her."

"Okay, we'll be there."

"Well," Isaiah says and looks directly at me. "Iz, I'll be outside to follow you home."

He backs away a few steps before turning around and walking out of the room. I can feel Finn's gaze on me, and I start to tingle under his scrutiny.

"I was hoping to get more time with you tonight."

Finn cups my cheek and I lean into his palm.

"Me too."

"I could come to your place," he suggests. "Get up early to head to the airport."

"As much as I would love that, I think you should go home." His face falls and I force a smile. "I just need some time alone. It's got nothing to do with you."

"Are you sure?"

I nod.

"You'll call me if you need anything?"

Again, I nod.

"Promise?"

I can't stop my lips from tugging up into a grin as I nod. Finn leans in and fuses his lips to mine. His hand settles on my hip and he pulls me into him, aligning my body with his. The last half hour melts away as sparks light me up from the inside out.

I feel air skate across my skin as Finn lifts my shirt and flattens his palm on my bare back to hold me close. My tongue collides with his to tangle in a fiery dance of need. Every single thing disappears until all that's left is us, our bodies, our passion.

And then, in a split second, it's gone. Finn ends the kiss and sets me away from him. My eyes open slowly to see him staring, his look dark and stormy.

"What's wrong?"

"I didn't want to stop."

"Then why did you?"

"Because if I didn't, I was going to take you against that wall," he nods to the space behind me. "And I wouldn't have given a damn if your brother was just outside or that now isn't the time. I'd have taken from you and I'm not at all sure I could've kept my wits about me to make sure you got what you needed."

"You'd have taken care of me."

"How do you know?"

"Because, Finn, you're not nearly as selfish as you make yourself out to be. And you care about me. A lot, I think. That fact alone would have made you take your time."

His expression shifts to one I don't see often: happiness. He leans in and presses his lips to my neck, just under my ear.

"I will fuck you, Izzy," he whispers, causing goosebumps to break out over my flesh. "When the time is right, I will fuck you and you're gonna beg me to give you more. You will always want more."

# 18

# FINN

*S*weat pours off my body and I swipe it from my face. Leaving Isabelle to come home alone was the last thing I wanted to do and not just because of the fire she ignited in my balls. She's dug her way past my defenses, past all the nasty bullshit I let build up over the last however many months and burrowed into my soul. When I'm not with her, I feel empty. I'm tired of feeling empty.

I take out all of my frustration with each jab of the punching bag that swings from the basement ceiling. It does little to cool the inferno in my blood but the ache that settles into my muscles slowly works its way into the forefront of my thoughts. After an hour of trying to ignore the firing synapses of my brain, I give up.

I limp to the bench and pick up my cell. A look at the screen tells me what I already know: Isabelle hasn't called or texted. Which means she's okay. Why then, can't I stop the worry that crees in?

*Because she means something to you. She's important.*

I wipe the beads of sweat from my face with a towel and hobble up the steps, closing and locking the basement door behind me. I'm not hiding the space but it's the one place I have completely to myself and keeping it locked makes me feel better.

When I reach the bathroom, I sit on the edge of the tub and take off my prosthetic, leaning it against the wall while I shower. I let the water heat until it's almost unbearable, knowing that's what it'll take to ease the tension. As it flows over my head, down my chest, I let my head fall back.

An image of Isabelle, straddling her Harley, enters my mind and instantly, my cock is hard. Unbearably so. I grip myself and squeeze and savor the way the pressure changes the image in my head. Isabelle splayed out on a bed, open and ready for me. Isabelle bent over her desk, legs spread. Isabelle kneeling before me, her mouth wrapped around my shaft, head bobbing and tongue caressing.

Bracing myself with an outstretched hand on the wall, I pump furiously, needing release. I force the image to change again… Izzy straddling my face, my tongue buried in her pussy.

The moment I start to think of her as Izzy, feisty, needy and in control, my leg shakes, and I struggle to hold myself upright as I explode. Regret slams into me the instant the haze clears. The first orgasm I've had since before the bombing should have been with her, not by my own hand.

I finish my shower quickly, washing the distaste down the drain. I reach past the shower curtain to grab a towel. After securing it around my waist, I sit on the ledge and swing my leg over until my foot is flat on the floor. I glare at the prosthetic, debating whether or not to put it on.

I opt to leave it off and instead, grab my cell phone off the bathroom counter. I hop to my bedroom, letting the towel fall to the floor before I collapse on the bed. I scoot to the middle and stare at the ceiling, wondering what Isabelle is doing.

I roll to my side and glance at the clock: two in the morning. Too late to call her, sure, but is it too late for a text? I open the texting app on my cell and stare at it, one second determined to send something and the next, talking myself out of it.

I drop my phone onto the nightstand and roll to my other side, away from temptation. I shift my thoughts to earlier in the day. The scene with Shane, and then the confrontation with Carson. Both men bring out the worst in me.

*Or maybe they bring out the best.*

Before Isabelle, I was bitter, enraged, broken. That's still there, deep within me, but Isabelle makes me want to do better, be better. And those men, the ones who are a threat but not a threat? They keep me sharp, focused, *determined.*

My eyes begin to drift closed as I think of all the ways my life has changed in such a short time and just as I'm about to give in to sleep, my cell phone pings, bringing me fully awake. I sit up and shift to pick up the phone.

My heartbeat quickens when I see the notification for a text and a grin spreads when I tap on the screen to read it.

**Isabelle: Are you awake?**

**Me: Yeah. Everything okay?**

**Isabelle: Can't sleep.**

**Me: Have you tried counting sheep?**

Her only response is a middle finger emoji. I lean back against the headboard and try to come up with something clever to say. Before I get the chance, my phone rings. I press the green button and put the phone to my ear.

"No sheep then?" I say by way of greeting.

"No sheep." Isabelle sounds tired. "How come you're awake?"

I inhale deeply, remembering my shower, and blow the air back out. I'm tired of lying to her, of lying to everyone, so a version of the truth is what comes out of my mouth.

"I jacked off in the shower and now I can't stop thinking of all the ways you'd feel better than my hand."

She huffs. "If you don't want to tell me, fine." There's a pout in her tone and I imagine her bottom lip poked out. "What time do you pick your mother up?"

"Seven." I look at the clock again, reminding myself of the time. "I'm pretty sure I'm not meant to sleep tonight."

"You could come here."

The hopeful lilt in her voice, mixed with the insecurity of not knowing how I'll respond is, surprisingly, a turn on.

"Then *you* wouldn't get any sleep."

"Or we both get sleep," she counters.

A chuckle rumbles out of me. "You and I both know that if I come over, there will be no chance of sleep and a very high chance that I won't make it to the airport on time."

"So, you'll come?"

"Be there in thirty."

I end the call and quickly make my way to the bathroom to put my prosthesis back on. I really need to give my stump a break, let it breath for a while, but that can wait. Isabelle can't. Once I'm dressed, I race out to my bike, as fast as I'm able.

I reach the gates of the Brotherhood property in twenty minutes and pull up to the booth, only to be greeted by a man I don't recognize.

"Pretty late for a social call," he says, a frown on his face.

I pull out my I.D. as Isaiah instructed me to do if I ever got held up at the gate. I hand it to the guy. He scans it and his scowl deepens.

"You here for Isabelle?"

"I am." I'm also not in the mood for the third degree. I certainly don't owe this guy any explanations.

He thrusts his hand out and I stare at it a moment before shaking it. "I'm Micah." He hands my license back to me. "Isabelle's father."

*Oh shit.*

"Nice to meet you, sir." I shift uncomfortably on my bike. "Izzy and I are just… we're, uh, working a case."

Micah throws his head back and laughs. "Son, if you're to the point where you're calling her Izzy and she's not clocking you for it, you're way past 'working a case'."

"No, sir." I clear my throat. "I assure—"

"Save it for someone a bit younger and more inexperienced than me." He doesn't appear angry, which makes me even more uncomfortable. "Isabelle is a grown woman and I'm not stupid. As long as you don't hurt her, I've got no issues with your… late night visits."

"Thank you, sir." It comes out sounding more like a question.

"And quit with the 'sir' shit," he snaps with no heat in his tone. "I founded this damn club and am no better, or worse, than you are. We're all equals here."

"Yes—" His eyes narrow. "Thanks, Micah."

He nods and opens the gate to allow me to pass. I straighten on my Harley, but before I can take off, he stops me with a parting shot.

"And son?" When he's sure he has my attention, he continues. "Hurt my baby girl and no amount of equality will be able to save your ass."

19

---

## ISABELLE

*I* pace the length of my living room, trying like hell to not look at the time again. It's been more than thirty minutes and Finn still isn't here. The moment he ended our phone call, I jumped out of bed and ran to the bathroom to do a quick refresh of my face and to make sure I was shaved perfectly in all the right places. I also changed the sheets on the bed, picked up all of the dirty clothes that hadn't made it to the hamper, and dug out the box of rubbers I have stashed in my nightstand.

Finally, I hear the rumble of his Harley as he nears my place. It's another two full minutes—I counted—before his footsteps hit my porch and another thirty seconds before he knocks on the door. I smooth my hands over the tank I'm wearing and wipe my sweaty palms on my shorts before opening the door.

"What took you so long?" I demand the second my eyes land on him.

I want to call the words back, yank them out of the air and pretend they don't exist. I have a tendency to speak before I think when I'm nervous and they simply popped out.

"I was making nice with your dad," he responds with a quirked brow.

"What? Why were you with—" I slap a hand over my mouth. Well, shit. "Omigod. He's on duty tonight. I totally forgot."

"Yeah, I figured," he chuckles. "Nothing quite like being derailed by the father of the woman you're meeting in the middle of the night."

"I am so sorry."

"Don't worry about it," he assures me. He looks past me, into the house. "You gonna let me in or are we standing here all night?"

I quickly step back to let him enter and close the door behind him. I notice a slight limp and wonder if his prosthesis is bothering him. I want to ask but don't, somehow recognizing that he needs to be the one to broach that subject.

"Can I get you anything to drink?"

He lifts his head and pins me with his stare. His eyes are swirling orbs of passion, dark and intense, and I fight the urge to look away. He stalks toward me, never breaking eye contact, and my thoughts turn to mush, my mouth dries up. A tingling sensation spreads through my body and settles at the juncture of my thighs.

When Finn reaches me, he brushes my hair out of my face and wraps his fingers around the side of my neck. He leans in and breathes into my ear, sending shivers down my spine.

"You," he whispers.

My lips part, I inhale sharply, time slows. I struggle to remember what I asked him but when I do, my mouth pulls into a sultry smile. Finn kisses me, once, twice, three times before lifting me into his arms.

"Bedroom?"

I nod in the right direction. As Finn carries me, he nips at my collarbone, my throat, my ear lobe. I tilt my head to grant him better access and the path he traces over my skin with his tongue feels like a promise of things to come.

Finn lays me down on the mattress and straightens. His face transforms from unchecked desire to doubt and I raise myself up onto my elbows.

"We don't have to do this." I want him, more than I've ever wanted anyone, but maybe I was wrong in thinking we wanted the same thing.

Finn's shoulders rise with a deep breath and he scrubs his hands over his face. "Izzy, I…"

I scoot to the end of the bed and tug him closer by the waistband of his jeans so he's standing between my legs. "Finn, what is it?"

He stares over me, at the wall, and is silent for so long I start to wonder if he's going to answer me, but he heaves a sigh and does.

"I haven't done this since…" he shrugs. "Well, since."

It hits me that he's concerned about his leg. In the heat of it all, I'd forgotten about it. For a brief moment, I forgot that sex with Finn might look a little different than what I'm used to. Knowing that how I react, what I say, can make or break what's happening between us, I relax my posture and pull him forward and twist, urging him to sit next to me.

"Are you worried about it?" The question feels stupid because clearly he is but I'm not sure how else to start this conversation.

"Fuck, yes, I'm worried about it," he snaps and then shakes his head. "Sorry. It's… I'm… What if I can't do it right?"

My unease lessens at his concern. This is something I can handle and with a fair amount of confidence that I won't screw it up.

"Finn, there is no right or wrong way. You know that,

right?" When he doesn't respond, I grip his chin and force him to look at me. "Right?"

He taps his head. "In here, intellectually, yes, I know that."

"Okay, good. Then what specifically are you worried about?" I ask, trying to get to the heart of the matter.

He stands and begins to pace, the limp I noticed earlier more pronounced. "Have you ever seen a stump? Have you ever really looked at a person's body when a piece of it is missing?"

"No," I answer honestly.

"It's not pretty on a good day," he snaps. "On a bad day? When the stump is chafed and red and sore, it's fucking ugly."

"And today is a bad day?"

He shrugs and paces away from me. Before he can get out of reach, I grab his hand and force him to stop. I stand and cup his cheeks in my hands so he has to look at me.

"Do you trust me?"

He narrows his eyes. "What?"

"You heard me. Do you trust me?"

"Of course I do. But what does that have to do with anything?"

"Everything."

I guide him to the bed and press down on his shoulders, forcing him to sit. He eyes me warily but doesn't resist. I drop to my knees in front of him and rest my hands on his thighs, slowly inching them toward his waist. His muscles bunch under my touch

I begin unbuckling his belt and then the button and zipper of his pants, and am surprised when I see he's not wearing anything under the denim. His cock is hard, thick, and begging to be freed. I swirl the tip of my finger around the mushroomed head and savor the way his body jerks in reaction.

"Lift yourself up," I demand in a breathy whisper.

Finn does and I pull his jeans over his hips and down his legs. I let them gather around his ankles, not wanting to take the time to remove his boots and socks. He, however, toes off the one boot and kicks his good leg free.

I brace my hands on the floor and lean down to let my lips graze his calf. I trace a path up to his knee, up his thigh and stop just short of my mouth touching his dick. When I lift my head, he groans. I switch my attention to the other side, the side he's worried about.

I press my lips to his inner thigh, and he twitches. As I slide down, closer to where his prosthesis joins with his stump, Finn wraps my hair around his fingers and tugs to get me to stop. Without looking at him, I grip his wrist and squeeze, silently telling him to let go. It takes a moment but his hold eases until he finally releases me.

"You don't have to do this," he says through what sounds like clenched teeth.

"I know."

I reach the prosthesis and lean back so I can look at it, really look at it. There's a thin strip of fabric that peeks out from the prosthesis and it appears that there's nothing tangible holding the leg in place. Beyond that, all I see when I look at it is a fascinating, intricate piece of equipment that allows Finn to be as normal—whatever that means—as possible.

I lift my head and look into his eyes. I see a bit of shame in them, and I hate that he feels that.

"Will you take it off for me?" I hold my breath while I wait for him to answer.

Without a word, he reaches forward and pulls the pros-thesis away from his body, presumably to loosen the suction that holds the prosthesis in place. I want to take it from him, hold it in my hands and study it, absorb it, revel in the detail and mechanics of how it operates, but this is for him, not me, so I let him set it off to the side.

I slip my fingers under the stump sock and peel it off, tossing it to the floor. Finn's residual limb is red and slightly chafed, just as he said it could be, but it's far from ugly. I press my lips just above where the limb ends, while simultaneously massaging his thigh. He flinches, his muscles spasm.

When, after a few minutes, he relaxes, I lift my eyes to him but leave my hands where they are.

"Does it hurt?"

He rolls his eyes as if he finds this whole process to be juvenile and pointless. "Yeah, it hurts." I yank my hands back, not wanting to cause him any pain. "No, Izzy. You touching it doesn't hurt. You touching anything on my body could never hurt." He inhales deeply. "But it aches all the time and is especially sore today."

Determined to make him forget about the pain, about his reservations and insecurities, I rise to my feet and pull his shirt up and over his head. Then I push him onto his back on the mattress and allow myself to take in the sight before me.

Finn's cock is long and my fingers itch to wrap around it, pump it until he explodes. I resist the urge, barely. His chest is smooth, sculpted, perfect. My eyes land on a tattoo on his left pec. The American flag appears to be blowing in the wind and there's an eagle perched with its talons wrapped around the pole. The words 'United we stand, Divided we fall' are inked underneath and the whole thing is somehow haunting. Finn has other tattoos on his arms, and I want to explore them, but later.

"You're killing me, Izzy." Finn's voice is strained.

I cross my arms and grab the hem of my own tank, pulling it up and over my head. I toss it to the floor and then quickly push my shorts over my hips to pool at my feet. I kick them to the side so I'm completely free.

Finn's sharp intake of breath spurs me on, and I lift a leg, intent on straddling him. Before I can, he uses his arms to scoot back toward the headboard, only stopping when the top of his head hits the tufted blue velvet.

"Come here," he commands with an outstretched hand.

I get on my knees, on the bed, and crawl my way up his body. I capture his lips in mine, thrusting my tongue to meet his, thrusting my hips so I can feel his cock against my clit. A moan escapes and he swallows it down.

Before I even realize what's happening, he breaks the kiss and lifts me so that I'm straddling his face, my pussy pulsating in anticipation.

"I do believe you offered me a drink."

My body bucks when he flattens his tongue on my clit and then swirls it around in tantalizing circles. I grip the top of the headboard to steady myself and let my head fall back on a groan.

His left hand remains on my hip while he uses his right to finger fuck me in perfect

rhythm with his tongue. When my hips undulate toward the sensation, he shifts his hand from my hip to my ass and pulls me closer, forcing my pussy to stay where he wants it, holding my body hostage.

"I'm so fucking thirsty."

His growl rumbles against my clit and it's all I can do not to explode right then and there. I don't want this to end. I never want it to end.

Finn feasts on me, drinks me in, sucks me dry until I'm a quivering mess above him. He curls the two fingers inside of me to tease my g-spot while never neglecting the assault on my clit. Within seconds of the erotic combination, my limbs shake uncontrollably, my knees tighten around his head, and a guttural moan tears out of me as I explode.

Before I can completely fall back to earth, Finn urges me

back and twists to reach for the box on the nightstand. In an effort to maintain the ecstasy high I'm riding, I reach down and circle my clit while he dons a rubber. When he's ready, he yanks my hand away and positions me to take his cock.

In one hard, smooth thrust, he impales me, and I feel my body stretching to accommodate him. Finn palms my tits and plays with my nipples as I ride him into oblivion. He glides in and out of me, thrusting, retreating, thrusting again. Each time his hips rise, I push my hips forward to accept all of him, to bury him deep.

My ears begin to ring, my vision blurs, sparks fly between us. Finn's hands haven't left my tits, so I grip his wrist and guide one hand down to my clit. Sensing what I want, he presses a thumb against the bundle of nerves and my pussy clamps around him.

"Fuck me, Finn," I shout and reach back to cup his balls. "Come with me."

Finn's body tenses and as my walls spasm, his cock pulsates, his release syncing with mine. I don't slow down, I don't let up, I don't fucking breathe as he shatters inside of me.

I collapse on top of him when I can no longer hold myself up and he wraps his arms around me and rolls us to the side. He brushes the sweat-dampened hair out of my face and leans forward to place a kiss to my lips.

"Holy shit," he whispers when he ends the kiss.

"Good holy shit or bad?" I ask, remembering how nervous he was earlier.

He tucks his chin in to look at me. "Amazing holy shit."

I smile and burrow into his side, not wanting to break the connection. I knew sex with Finn would be phenomenal but that was a whole new level. Not wanting to analyze that at the moment, I close my eyes and simply savor the feel of him next to me.

He rubs my back for a while, the motion soothing, relaxing. Before long, my eyelids become too heavy to open and I have to fight the sleep that's threatening to take over.

"What time do you have to leave?" I ask after an exhausted yawn.

"Around five."

I lift my head to look at the clock on the nightstand and see that it's almost four. "I'm sorry."

"For what?"

"You're gonna be exhausted when you pick your mom up."

"Izzy, it was worth every second." He kisses the top of my head. "Get some sleep. I'll wake you up before I go."

Another yawn escapes and I raise up onto my elbow. "Or," I grin. "We could find ways to stay awake."

His smile is wide. "Well, damn."

"What?" I ask, confused.

"I'm going to lose a lot of sleep over the years, aren't I?"

# 20

# FINN

*P*assenger after passenger walks through the tunnel from the plane to the terminal, not one of them my mother. I lean against the wall, arms crossed over my chest, and continue to wait impatiently while staring at the floor. I don't want to be here. Don't get me wrong, I'm happy to see my mom, but leaving Isabelle in bed this morning was one of the hardest things I've done in recent memory.

"Finnigan!"

I lift my head in time to see my mom launch herself at me with outstretched arms. I catch her easily and twirl her around in a hug, ignoring the twinge of pain in my leg. When I set her on her feet, I notice tears streaking her perfectly applied makeup.

"Mom, don't cry," I urge, wiping her tears away.

She swats at me. "I'll cry if I want to, Finnigan."

"You should be happy right now, Mom, not sad."

"I am happy."

She pats my cheek, the action made harder by the incredible height difference between us. I've never understood that about women, that crying because they're happy thing. It makes no sense to me, but I stopped trying to make sense of females a long time ago.

We start to walk to baggage claim and that's when it hits me. I'm glad my mom is here. When I saw her, hugged her, relief settled into my bones. I wasn't expecting that. I was counting on the familiar bitterness coloring the moment, but it didn't.

"What are you smiling about, Finnigan?"

I look down at my mother and realize she's right, I am smiling. "Nothing. I'm just happy to see you."

"You sound shocked by that."

"I am," I say honestly. Determined to be as honest with her as I can, I add, "I love you, Mom. You know that. But these last two years have been hard. I haven't wanted to see anyone, deal with life… none of it."

"What's changed?"

I think about how to answer that and settle on, "Everything."

Two hours later, we're pulling into my driveway. I get out and open my Mom's door for her and then the trunk to get her luggage. She's assured me that, despite the sheer amount of luggage, she's only staying for a week. How much stuff does she need to get through seven days?

By the time I have everything unloaded, she's sitting on the couch with her feet propped up on the coffee table. She pats the cushion next to her and I sit. She lifts my hand and holds it in her lap, much like she's done my entire life when she's about to get serious, or emotional.

"Finnigan, your home is lovely."

I look around the room, see all of the furniture that Isabelle helped me pick out, that the guys helped put into place, and smile.

"Thank you." I laugh self-consciously. "I had help."

"Oh?" She raises her brows in question. "From who?"

"Friends," I say but it feels like an inadequate way to describe them all. "No, that's not quite true." I lean back and try to put my thoughts into words. "They're more than that. Yes, they're friends, but they're becoming family, my family here, in Indiana."

"And who are 'they'?"

"The Broken Rebel Brotherhood. They're a group of veterans who came together and created a motorcycle club. They help people who the system fails. You're gonna meet them tonight, at dinner, and I know you'll love them."

Her face falls slightly. "So, no girls? No special someone in your life?"

I realize she's focused in on the word 'brotherhood' and misinterpreted it, as I'm sure many do.

"Trust me, Mom, there are women there. Just as many women as men."

"Well, that's something, I suppose." She pats my hands. "And as long as you're happy, I can wait for the rest to happen."

I debate whether or not to tell her about Isabelle. Part of me wants to be selfish and keep Isabelle all to myself but the son in me hates to see the disappointment on my mother's face.

"There is someone," I mumble.

Mom perks up immediately. "Oh?"

I shake my head and chuckle. "Her name is Isabelle and she's also a member of the club. Her dad actually founded it back in the day."

"And will I get to meet this Isabelle at dinner?"

"You will."

"Good." She rises from the couch and stretches her arms over her head. "I think I'll take a nap if you don't mind. That flight really took it out of me."

"Of course." I stand and wrap my arm around her shoulders. "I'll show you where you'll be sleeping."

I get my mom settled and return to the living room. I hear her shuffling around the room but it's not long before the door clicks shut and noise ceases. I flop onto the couch and begin to worry.

Mom has never been one to take naps. She's always on the go and, as far as I know, still has an active social life. I glance toward the spare bedroom. The last two years have aged her, and I can't help but feel responsible. Losing my dad was hard on her and then to essentially lose me too? I can't imagine the pain she's felt.

I vow to myself to make up for lost time, to appreciate every minute I have with her, to never take her for granted. I, more than most, know that everything can change in the blink of an eye… or the explosion of a bomb.

Lost in thought, it takes a moment for it to sink in that my phone is ringing. I shake my head and pull it out of my pocket. When I see that it's Isaiah, my stomach plummets.

"Is Izzy okay?" I ask as soon as I answer.

Isaiah laughs. "Brother, you've got it bad."

"Answer me," I bark, not in the mood for his good-natured ribbing.

"Yeah, she's fine. That's not why I'm calling."

Relief hits me fast and hard, but it takes a few seconds for my heart to settle into a normal rhythm. "What's up?"

"I hate to ask this of you, but can you meet me at the hospital? I know your mom is in town, but I wouldn't have called if I had any other choice."

"The hospital?"

"Yep. Ann's there, getting checked out before going to the police station. Apparently, Carson showed up at her house this morning, demanding to see their son, and when she refused, he beat the shit out of her."

"Fuck," I mumble, trying to wrap my brain around the information.

"She called and asked that we go to the police station with her. She's understandably scared." He pauses. "And she asked for you specifically."

"What? Why?"

"I don't know. I think she feels safest with you because you were the one that sat down with her that night at the bar. You were the first one to make sure she was okay. That stays with a person, ya know?"

I nod and then realize he can't see me. "Yeah, right."

"So, think you can do this? If not, I'll figure something out, but I thought it couldn't hurt to ask."

Again, I glance toward the room my mother is sleeping in. I hate to wake her up, knowing that if she's napping, she really is tired. I also can't leave her alone. Not with everything going on.

"Is there anyone you can spare to come sit at my place while we go? I can't leave my mom alone."

"Of course. I'll send Tillie and Ruby over. I'd send Iz but something tells me she needs to get some sleep. I heard she had a visitor last night." There is no judgement, no censure in his tone. Just a teasing quality that I've missed from my time in the military. "As soon as they get there, head to the hospital. I'll wait by the ER entrance for you."

"Thanks. See ya in a bit."

Isaiah ends the call and I go to check on my mom. I open the door quietly and see her lying on the bed, an afghan I recognize as one she knitted years ago, on top of her. No wonder she has so much luggage. She brought her own damn blankets.

Satisfied that she's okay, I take a minute to write her a note, explaining where I'm at. I gather my wallet and keys, as well as my pistol, and wait for Tillie and Ruby to arrive. They do within twenty minutes and once I've reassured myself that my mom is in good hands, I take off for the hospital.

The drive to the hospital seems to take forever when in reality, it's only about fifteen minutes. I see Isaiah standing at the entrance, as he said he would be, and I park my Harley next to his at the far end of the parking lot. When I reach him, he nods.

"Thanks for coming. Sorry to have to call you away from family."

"As you've tried to get me to see several times, you're family too. It's all good, brother."

Isaiah grins before turning away and striding inside, leaving me to follow. Within seconds, a slender woman with graying hair walks up to Isaiah and gives him a hug. Her scrubs tell me she's a nurse but other than that, I haven't a clue who she is.

When she steps back, she turns to me and sticks out her hand for me to shake. "Hi, Finn. I'm Emersyn, Doc's wife. We haven't had the pleasure of meeting yet."

"Nice to meet you."

"I just wish it were under better circumstances." She smirks at Isaiah. "These guys keep me on my toes and their cases give me job security."

"We only do it because we love you, Em."

Isaiah winks at her and a twinge of envy hits me. Will I ever get to the point where I'm this comfortable with all of them? Where the family bond is so cemented into the moments of every day that I never have to worry when it will fall apart? I hope so.

"Right," she laughs. "I'll take you to Ann."

Emersyn leads us to an actual room and not a curtained off cubicle that is so indicative of emergency rooms. Before she opens the door, she turns, and her face is all business.

"I don't know what happened to her, but I do know

there's something about her version of events that doesn't quite sit right with me."

"What do you mean?"

She shrugs. "It's just a gut feeling. Isaiah, you know how many victims of domestic violence I've tended to over the years, not to mention the work I do with the club. I can't pinpoint it with Ann, but I'm telling you, tread carefully."

"Thanks for the heads up."

Emersyn rests her hand on Isaiah's forearm when he reaches for the doorknob. "And brace yourself. I trust my gut but that doesn't mean that her injuries aren't severe." She looks down and when she lifts her head, her eyes are glistening with unshed tears. "They remind me so much of the first time I saw Red."

"Who's Red?" I ask, confused.

Isaiah's jaw ticks and his face becomes red with rage. "My mother."

# 21

## ISABELLE

"So, you're the woman my son is in love with?"

The question is jarring and while I'm trying to process her use of the word 'love', Tillie and Ruby are laughing like idiots at the end of the bar at the main house.

*Did Finn tell his mother that he loves me? Does he love me?*

I have no answers, nor are they questions I'm going to ask.

"I'm Isabelle," I say before taking a long pull of my beer.

She looks me up and down, glances at the beer bottle in my hands, and smiles. "You'll do."

The laugh that bubbles up my throat causes me to almost choke and spit beer in this poor woman's face. I slap a hand over my mouth to stop the disaster and feel the liquid dribble down my chin, into my lap.

*Way to go, Iz. Great first impression.*

Finn's mother reaches into her purse and pulls out a handkerchief and hands it to me.

"Here," she says. "Clean yourself up and we'll chat."

I wipe my mouth off and then my hands. I set the used handkerchief down and spot the initials H.W. embroidered on the corner. Mrs. Walsh must catch me staring and offers an explanation.

"Hank Walsh. He was my husband, God rest his soul."

"I'm sorry."

She flaps her hand. "Oh, pish. I lost him years ago. I miss him like the dickens and carry that around because it makes me feel like I have a piece of him with me all the time. He always had it in his pocket, no matter what."

"I'll wash it for you."

She lifts it and puts it back in her purse. "A little beer never hurt nothing." She snaps her purse closed. "My Hank loved a good lager. Why, he'd be thrilled that his son found someone who can appreciate the taste of a cold one."

I can't help but smile. She has a way of calming even the worst of nerves. "Now, what are your intentions with my Finnigan?"

Or not.

"I…" I glance at Tillie and Ruby who are watching us intently, and then return my attention to the spitfire in front of me. "I don't think this is a conversation I should be having with you before I even have it with Finn."

Her stare doesn't waver, and I feel like a bug under a microscope the way she's studying me. Finally, she nods. "Fair enough. Tell me about yourself then."

I shake my head, trying to keep up with her quick shifts. "What do you want to know?"

"You've already told me you won't talk about what I want to know," she retorts sweetly. "So, tell me what you're willing to tell me."

"Oh, um… okay." I prop my head on my hand. "I'm a trauma counselor. I do a lot of work within the club, with the victims we help. I also work with Wounded Warriors. That's where Finn and I met."

"Was it love at first sight?"

I laugh. "You're tenacious, you know that?"

"I do," she confirms. "So, was it?"

I heave a sigh. "I almost ran him over with my Harley so I'm going to say no, it wasn't love at first sight. I think it was more like him trying to control himself so he didn't kill me."

"Sounds like my Finnigan. Quick to anger since the bombing." She tsks like only a mother can and then pins me with her stare again. I swallow hard, bracing myself for whatever is going to come out of her mouth next. "But you're in love with him now, aren't you?"

Before I can respond, I catch sight of Finn and Isaiah as they step through the door. I stand on the rung of the barstool and wave them over. Mrs. Walsh looks over her shoulder and sighs, loudly.

"Don't think I'll be forgetting that I still need an answer to my question."

"Yes, ma'am."

"Mom, quit terrorizing my girlfriend," Finn says as soon as he's within earshot.

My eyes widen and he looks at me like he's as shocked as I am at the words that he spoke. We've never put a label on us, not that we've been together long enough to think about labels. Hell, we haven't even known each other long. But 'girlfriend' feels right. It's how I see myself in relation to Finn if I stop and think about it.

"I'm not terrorizing her, Finnigan." She glances at me. "Am I, Isabelle?"

I vigorously shake my head. "No, ma'am."

"Oh, stop with the ma'am stuff. Makes me feel every bit of my age. I'm Margaret. You can call me that or Mama. Either is fine with me."

"Okay. Thanks."

This day keeps getting weirder and weirder. I'm trying to run with it, to enjoy it, but now that Finn's here, all I want to do is launch myself into his arms and demand he take me to my place and get me naked. And those are not thoughts I need to have with his mother present.

"I'm sorry I was gone when you woke up," Finn says to his mom.

"It's fine, Finnigan. Tillie and Ruby were great. They explained everything your note didn't."

I see Finn clench his jaw and wonder how much he left out of the note, how much Tillie and Ruby said that maybe they shouldn't have. At least not without consulting with Finn first.

"Is the client okay? The woman you went to see in the hospital? Ann, I think they said her name is."

Finn's eyes dart back and forth between me and his mother and he finally focuses on her. "Uh, yeah, she'll be okay."

"Good." She reaches up and pats his shoulder. "That's good." She uses Finn's arm for balance as she gets down from the barstool. "Now, can someone please show me to the restroom? My bladder isn't what it used to be."

Tillie and Ruby rush over then and lead Margaret to the bathroom, leaving Finn and I alone. I appreciate it because I've got questions... so many questions.

"What aren't you saying about Ann?" I waste no time, not sure how much we have.

"Do we have to do this now?"

"Yes, we do. Not only is it bad form to keep secrets from your *girlfriend*, it's also never a good idea to keep them from the club. I'm part of the club. So talk."

"I don't know what to say. It's weird. The whole situation feels off."

"How so?" I ask, tilting my head.

"When we got to the ER, Emersyn told us that she didn't necessarily believe Ann's story about her injuries. And then she said they reminded her of your mom's the first time she saw her."

I shiver, remembering pictures I've seen over the years. Our parents tried to keep the details from Isaiah and me, but we were brats and went snooping. Besides, when the club was handed over to our generation, we were granted access to all files, including those of the founding members and their spouses. I can't say I regret seeing the pictures, only that my mother suffered the way she did.

"Did you see Ann? Talk to her?"

"Of course."

"And what does your gut tell you?"

"That Emersyn is on to something." He shrugs. "Like her, I can't pinpoint exactly what, but both Isaiah and I struggled to believe everything she said."

"Did she follow through with going to the police station and filing a report?"

He nods. "She did. Gave the cops the same story. Also told them where to find Carson so they were able to pick him up on charges of assault and battery and he's locked up for now."

"Well, at least she's safe while we try to sort it all out," I say. Finn's eyes narrow. "What?"

"Carson didn't have a scratch on him, Izzy. Someone beat the living hell out of Ann and to hear her tell it, she fought back, or tried to. Whoever did that to her would have defensive wounds, scratches on their hands and arms. Bruised knuckles. *Something*." He shakes his head. "Not a single mark on him."

"Okay. If it wasn't Carson, who was it? His friends from the bar?"

"Maybe. Probably," he concedes as he shoves his hands through his hair. "I don't fucking know, and I hate that. Between the unknown threat to you and now this... I just don't know."

I lean into him and wrap my arms around his waist. "We'll figure it out."

"I know but I don't like it. Any of it. My gut says it's all connected but I can't figure out how."

We stand there, holding onto each other. Finn rubs circles over my back and I listen to his racing heartbeat thump against my cheek. I have no idea how long we stand like that, but we're jolted apart by his mother's voice.

"And there's my answer."

# 22

# FINN

"That was fun."

I take my eyes off the road and glance at my mother. Isabelle told us to take the club Jeep home since all I had was my Harley. My mom has no problem with me riding but has sworn up and down she'll never be 'caught dead on that hunk of metal'.

"It was."

"I like Isabelle. And the rest of them. But especially Isabelle."

My mother isn't subtle. Never has been.

"I like her too."

"What is it with your generation and your fear of the word 'love'?" she asks with a bite to her tone.

"I don't fear it, Mom."

"Then why don't you use it?" I can feel her eyes on me while I navigate the dark country roads.

"Because, Mom, I don't..." I close my mouth letting my words trail off.

I don't know why I don't use the word. Maybe because for so long I've thought of myself as unlovable. Or maybe because I'm afraid that if I put words to what I'm feeling, it'll disappear.

"Finnigan, I'm going to ask you the same thing I asked Isabelle. Do you love her?"

"What was her answer?" I ask in an effort to stall.

"We were interrupted before she could tell me. But she loves you."

"How do you know?"

"A mother knows."

I roll my eyes, grateful that she can't see them in the dark interior of the Jeep.

"Well?" she prods.

"Well what?"

She sighs dramatically. "Do you love Isabelle?"

I realize that the question doesn't require as much thought as I assumed it would.

"Yeah, Mom, I love her."

"Then why in heaven haven't you told her that?"

"Because we just met. It's all still very new."

"So," she counters. "You know as well as anyone that tomorrow is guaranteed. Tell her, Finnigan. Sooner rather than later. Don't let this be one more thing that gets in your way of living. Don't let not telling her be another regret."

The rest of the drive is made in silence. By the time I pull into the driveway, my mom's soft snoring fills the vehicle. I sit there for a few minutes, hating to wake her. It's been such a long day for her, having boarded a plane in the wee hours of the morning, navigating layovers and then meeting everyone here and dinner at the club. She's been a good sport about it, and I know she had a good time, but it doesn't ease the guilt I feel for wearing her out.

I rest my hand on her shoulder and gently shake her. "We're home, Mom."

She startles awake and stifles a yawn. "Oh my. I'm sorry, I fell asleep."

"It's okay, Mom. I'm sorry I kept you out so late."

She waves away my concern. As she unbuckles her seatbelt, I exit the Jeep and walk around to open her door and help her to the house. Once she's settled on the couch, I'm finally able to relax. I sit in the overstuffed chair and start working on taking my prosthesis off, needing the relief.

When I set it on the floor next to me, I catch sight of my mom staring.

"Is everything okay, Mom?" Her eyes well with tears and she doesn't answer. "Mom?" I prod, concerned.

Her eyes snap to mine. "What?"

"Are you okay?"

"Yes, of course. It's just..." She shakes her head. "This is the first time I've seen you take that off. You're so convincing that I forget about it completely."

I realize then that my running halfway across the country may have been the right thing for me, but it certainly didn't help her any. I lost a leg, yes, but she lost something too. I can't imagine what she felt seeing her son go through what I've gone through.

"Do you have any questions about it?" I ask, unsure how to go about talking about it with her.

"Does it hurt? Do you still hurt from the bombing?"

"Mostly it's phantom pain." She nods in understanding. "The stump does hurt sometimes. But I handle it."

"Does Isabelle know about it?"

I can't stop the chuckle that crawls up the back of my throat. Leave it to my mom to bring all things back to the woman in my life.

"She does."

"Good." She stands from the couch. "I'm going to bed. I'm exhausted."

"Do you need anything?"

She closes the distance between us and leans over to kiss my cheek. "No Finnigan. I've got everything I need. Thank you."

"Night, Mom. Love you."

"Good night, sleep tight. Don't let the bedbugs bite," she chirps as she did every single night when she'd tuck me into bed as a boy. "I love you, too."

I remain in the chair and listen to the familiar sounds of my mother brushing her teeth, the toilet flushing, doors opening and closing as she readies for bed. When I'm satisfied that she's settled in for the night, I stand and hop to the kitchen for a drink.

I grab a beer out of the fridge and twist the top off. I take a long pull and savor the cold as it glides down my throat. I finish that drink and grab a second before making my way back to the couch. As I sit down, I feel my phone vibrate in my pocket. I pull it out to see who's texting me.

**Isabelle: I like your mom.**

I smile and take a sip before responding.

**Me: She likes you.**

**Isabelle: What about you?**

**Me: I like my mom too.**

Isabelle responds with a laughing emoji and one sticking its tongue out. I knew that's not what she meant but I can't seem to resist the urge to tease her.

**Isabelle: That's not what I meant.**

**Me: I know.**

**Isabelle: ???**

**Me: I like you too.**

**Isabelle: I wish you were here.**

Before I can respond, a text from another number comes through and a quick check tells me it's from Ann. The hairs on my neck stand up.

**Ann: I'm scared. I keep hearing noises, like someone is in my house.**

I fire off a quick text to Isaiah, alerting him to the fact that I've heard from Ann and he responds, instructing me to get screenshots. Only after that do I respond to Ann.

**Me: Have you called 911?**

**Ann: No. Can you come over and check things out? The police never take me seriously.**

I think back over her statement this afternoon and can't help but agree with her. Maybe they have similar suspicions that her story just doesn't add up. And if she is a victim like she says she is, I'll have to deal with the guilt of my doubt.

**Me: I'll send someone from the club over.**

**Ann: I don't know them. Please, Finn?**

My phone rings before I can respond to Ann. It's Isabelle.

"Where did you go?" she asks when I answer the call.

"Sorry, Ann started texting me. She says she thinks there could be someone in her house. I'm not buying it but she's asking me to come over and check."

"And you can't leave your mom," Isabelle says. "I'll go."

"What? No, you can't go alone."

"Why not? It's not like she's gonna hurt me. She's battered as it is. I'll stop by and check things out and then let you know what I find."

"Your brother will kill me if anything happens to you."

"Nothing is going to happen, Finn. Besides, it's not like I haven't done stuff like this hundreds of times over the years. I may have backed off on my club duties but I'm still a voting member and I don't always need permission for things."

I can hear the annoyance in her voice and against my better judgement, I cave. "Fine. But you text me when you get there and when you leave." I inhale deeply. "Better yet, call me when you get there and put the phone on speaker so I can hear everything that's going on."

"Fine," she grumbles and ends the call.

I slam my phone on the arm of the chair and then immediately pick it back up. I send Isaiah another text letting him know what his stubborn sister is doing. I'll ask for forgiveness later.

I also send a text to Ann telling her I'll be right over. I don't bother telling her it'll be Isabelle instead of me because I'm not in the mood to argue with her. If she's scared, it shouldn't matter who's coming.

Satisfied that I've sent all the required texts, I sit there, phone in hand, and wait.

# 23

## ISABELLE

*I* knock on Ann's door again. I've been knocking for five minutes already with no luck. I send off a quick text to Finn and ask him to text Ann saying he's at the door. If my suspicions are right, she'll open up if she thinks it's him. Then I stand there, ignoring the rumble of the Harley down the street.

I caught sight of someone following me not long after I left BRB property. I haven't been able to make out who it is but if I had to guess, I'd say it's Isaiah. He's the only one, other than Finn apparently, to blatantly ignore my wishes. My anger spiked knowing that Finn went behind my back but that's a problem for some other time. Right now, I need in this house, and then I need to go home.

I glance over my shoulder toward my own bike and jump when the door finally opens. I whirl back around and am shocked to see Ann standing there, clad in only a lacy bra and panties, her eyes swollen and her face bruised. Damn, someone did a number on her.

"What are you doing here?" she asks. She leans out to

look around me and sighs when she realizes I'm alone. "I thought Finn was coming."

"He wanted to come but he's got family in town. I'm sure you understand." I force a smile. "He asked if I'd come make sure everything was okay."

Ann tries to close the door in my face, but I stick my hand out to stop her. She glares at me. "Everything is fine."

"Do you mind if I come in, see for myself? It's our policy that when a client feels like they're not safe, we don't leave any stone unturned." When she doesn't acquiesce, I rush to add, "Finn would kill me if I didn't check everything. He's worried about you."

Finally, she opens the door and steps aside for me to enter. I look back down toward the other Harley, suddenly glad I was followed. Ann is giving me very weird vibes and I'm beginning to question my sanity for insisting I come alone.

Assured that if I don't come back out in a reasonable amount of time, someone will come looking for me, I step over the threshold. Ann yanks off a blanket that's draped over the back of the couch and wraps it around herself. Her movements don't seem slowed or hampered any by her injuries.

"Finn said you thought you heard someone in the house?"

She brushes her hair out of her face. "Yeah."

I wait to see if she'll elaborate but she doesn't. "Okay. Well, I'll take a look around. Check all the windows and doors, make sure locks are secure. I'm guessing it was just the wind or normal settling of the house causes some creaks, but it never hurts to be sure."

"Are you calling me stupid?"

I rear back at her question. I have no idea what could possibly have made her make that mental leap. "No, I'm not."

"You think it didn't already cross my mind that it could

have been the wind or normal 'creaking'?" She uses air quotes and I find it annoying.

"I'm sure you did. Obviously you dismissed those ideas because you reached out to Finn because you were scared. I'm only here to help, Ann."

"I didn't ask for your help," she snaps.

"But you did. You asked for the club's help. I'm part of the club. I may not be who you wanted to show up tonight but I'm who you got."

She flops down on the couch. "Do what you have to do. And then get out. I've got a long day tomorrow and need to get some sleep."

Why the hell is she acting like I'm inconveniencing her? Is her fear getting the best of her or is there more to the story? I ponder all of this as I methodically make my way through the house, room by room.

When I reach what I assume is her son's bedroom, I find it odd that he's not in it, asleep like a young boy should be at this hour. I dismiss the concern rather quickly though. She was clearly beat up earlier so maybe her son is with his grandparents or something.

After securing the interior, I make my way outside via a sliding door that leads to a back patio. I walk around the perimeter, shining my cell's flashlight on the ground as I do. When I reach a window on the side of the house, I see a pile of cigarette butts. Ann doesn't smoke, at least not that I know of. Neither does Carson. Who, then, was standing here? Judging by the pile, they weren't here for a short period of time, either.

I take a picture and also pick one of the butts up and put it in a plastic baggie in my pocket. I remembered to grab some as I was leaving my house, just in case I found anything that needed to be tested as evidence.

I tip my head back and look at the side of the house,

trying to picture the interior layout so I can have an accurate picture in my mind of what these windows lead to. One is the downstairs half bath while another is over the kitchen sink. The two windows to the second level would be in the master bedroom and the spare bedroom.

I make my way back inside and find Ann standing in the kitchen, a whiskey glass in her hand. She downs the amber liquid when she sees me and sets the empty glass in the sink.

"Let me guess," she says. "You didn't find anything?"

It strikes me as odd, the way she words that question. Almost as if she knew I wouldn't find anything. Again, I dismiss my concerns. Clearly someone was here. The cigarette butts are proof of that. Maybe they weren't here tonight, and this is all a ploy to get Finn here, but that doesn't mean that the threat to her and her son isn't real.

"Actually, I did find something." Her eyes widen. "Know anyone who smokes Marlboro Reds?"

She shakes her head, a little too fast. She's hiding something. But what?

"Okay. I'll take what I have and get it tested. It shouldn't be long before we have enough to keep Carson behind bars for a very long time."

I stick with the original story she gave us, even though I'm relatively sure it's not Carson who's her problem. I trust Finn and he's been adamant that Carson as a suspect doesn't necessarily fit.

When she says nothing, I start toward the front door. I turn to her before leaving. "You're safe for tonight, Ann. I didn't find anything to suggest that anyone was inside. I'll have a club member posted outside, just to be on the safe side."

"Weren't you already doing that?" she asks.

"We were but pulled them tonight when Carson was arrested. I'll get someone back here before I leave."

"Ask Finn," she suggests. "He'll come."

Victim or not, this chick is delusional.

"I already explained to you, Ann, that he can't." I open the front door and step outside. "Try to get some sleep. You'll be safe. I promise."

I close the door behind me and descend the steps as quickly as I can, distancing myself from the crazy. Rather than go to my Harley, which is parked at the curb, I walk down the street toward the person who followed me. The closer I get, the more convinced I am of who it is.

"What the fuck, Isaiah?" I whisper harshly. No need to wake the neighbors.

"Iz, don't start with me."

"Do you all really trust me that little?"

"It's not you we don't trust," he counters angrily. "Or are you forgetting that the last time you were here you were shot?"

"How could I forget?" I yank the hem of my jacket and shirt up to expose the wound. "I've got a permanent reminder."

Isaiah's eyes darken. "I needed to know you were okay. I trust you to do the job, Iz, and I'm sorry for making you think otherwise. But I'm not sorry for giving a shit about you. And I'm sure Finn isn't either."

My anger deflates. Isaiah has always been protective of me. That's nothing new. And Finn? I'm learning that he's equally protective.

"You need to get someone here to sit watch tonight," I inform Isaiah. I pull the baggie out of my pocket. "I don't believe for a second that there was anyone inside the house, but someone's been watching her."

He takes the baggie from me and tucks it into his jacket. "I'll have Noah or Jace come and sit."

I nod.

"Iz, go home. Get some sleep."

"What are you going to do?"

"I'll wait here for one of the guys to arrive and then I'm going home to sleep next to my wife."

"Are you going to call Finn and fill him in, or should I?"

"I will," he says quickly. "I'm pretty sure you need to cool down before you talk to him." I roll my eyes. "What? I like the guy. He did the right thing, and I don't want him second-guessing himself because you're butt-hurt."

"Fine," I snap.

I turn to walk away but he stops me.

"Iz?"

I look over my shoulder at him.

"Love you."

"Love you, too."

# 24

# FINN

*B*race yourself for Iz's wrath.

That's what Isaiah texted me last night, after Isabelle left Ann's house. I have yet to hear from Isabelle herself but if she waits much longer, she's not the only one that will be unleashing their anger.

"Still haven't heard from her?"

I glance up from my phone toward my mother. She's made herself at home in my kitchen and the smells that are coming from the pots on the stove are making my mouth water.

"Not a damn word," I grumble.

"Language, Finnigan." She points the wooden spoon in her hand at me. "You're not too old for me to use this on you, just remember that."

I'd like to see her try to bend me over her knee. The image that forms in my mind is the comical relief I need to stop waiting, silently demanding my phone to ring.

"Still not telling me what you're making?" I ask.

"If you haven't figured it out by now then you've definitely been away from home for far too long."

I step up behind her and look over her shoulder. She pushes me back with her hip. "No cheating."

"Well, it's not your spaghetti. Not red enough. And it's not pot roast because you make that in the crock pot, not on the stove." I take in all the ingredients scattered over the counter and it hits me. "It's your Irish stew."

She lifts a bite out of the pot and blows on it before holding it out for me. "Here, taste it."

The savory stew coats my tongue and melts in my mouth. "Mmmmm."

"Good?"

"Delicious."

"I'll teach your Isabelle the recipe. She should be able to make it for you."

"Mom," I say in a warning tone.

"Don't 'Mom' me. Is it so wrong that I want you happy?"

"Of course not. But I can handle my own love life."

"Apparently not, judging by the way you've been sulking around here all day, obsessively checking your phone."

Before I can argue with her, there's a knock on my door. I weave through the living room and look through the peephole to see the top of Isabelle's head. Before yanking the door open, I step back and take a deep breath.

"Finn, I heard you," she calls through the door. "Let me in."

"Finnigan, let the poor girl in," my mom demands simultaneously from the kitchen.

I open the door and turn away from Isabelle, leaving her standing there.

"What is your problem?"

I whirl on her, stalk toward her until I need to lean down to get in her face. "You, Izzy. You're my problem. Do you have any idea how worried I was about you last night? And all because you got pissed that I did what I felt I needed to do to keep you safe, you've shut me out."

"I'm sorry."

"Not only did you go off half cocked and…" I close my mouth, open it again. "What?"

Isabelle smiles. "I said, I'm sorry."

"Oh."

"You're right, I was livid when I noticed Isaiah following me. And I was still livid when I left Ann's house. Which is why I took the time to calm down and think things through before I came over here, *half cocked* as you put it, and rip you a new one."

"Well, I'm glad you see things my way."

"That's not what I said." She stabs a finger in my chest, no longer apologetic. "I'm still angry." She shakes her head. "No, that's not right. I'm hurt, Finn. I'm hurt that you don't trust me to be smart, to be careful, to handle things I've been handling for years without you."

"I trust you, Izzy. I don't trust everyone else."

"That's very similar to what Isaiah said when I flipped on him last night."

"It's familiar because it's true." I wrap my fingers around her wrist and hold her hand to my chest. "You are smart, Izzy. Smart, beautiful, stubborn, capable, strong-willed. And you're also very loved, so much so that people worry about you and will do whatever it takes to make sure you're safe, your anger be damned."

"Are you saying what I think you're saying?"

"That I'm one of those people who love you?" She nods. "Yeah, I am. I love you, Izzy. I think I fell a little bit in love with you the first time I heard you say 'fuck'. You were not at all what I was expecting."

"Neither were you."

I kiss the top of her head. "I love you and I'll never, *ever* stop doing what I feel I need to do to protect you. You might as well accept that, if you plan on spending any amount of time with me."

"I love you, too, Finn. And I'll try to deal with your over-protectiveness as long as you promise to accept the fact that there are times I'm going to do things that worry you. It's not on purpose. But I can't change who I am."

"I wouldn't want you to."

"I can see I'm interrupting something."

I lift my head and Isabelle whirls around to see Ann standing in the doorway. Only then do I realize that we left it open.

"Ann, what are you doing here?" Isabelle asks before I can force any words out.

"You said he had company. That he had family visiting." She lifts the casserole dish in her hands. "I was trying to be nice."

"Oh dear." I look to see my mom standing just behind me. "I'm not sure I have enough food for all your friends."

"Don't worry about it, Mom," I assure her before she can work herself into a tizzy. "Ann was only stopping by for a minute." I focus on Ann. "Isn't that right?"

Before Ann can respond, Isabelle steps toward her. "I'll see you out, Ann. Now isn't really a good time."

Ann shifts away from Isabelle and sets the dish on the entry table by the door. "I can see myself out."

With that, she turns and practically runs to her car. Isabelle and I exchange a glance, fully aware that my mom is still in the room. Mom makes her way toward the door and lifts the tin foil off the dish.

"Chicken noodle casserole." She recovers the food and looks at me. "Think she poisoned it?"

Isabelle snorts but I manage to hold back my reaction. "Why would she poison it?" I ask.

"Didn't seem quite right, that girl." She lifts the dish, carries it to the kitchen, and a loud thud reverberates as she tosses the whole thing in the trash. When she turns back around, she rests her hands on her hips. "There. Now, who's hungry? The stew is ready."

"We'll be there in a minute, Mom."

"I'll set the table." She starts to pull dishes from the cabinets. "If you two need to talk in private, feel free to go to your room, Finnigan. The food will be here when you're ready."

Summarily dismissed, Isabelle and I go to my room. I shut the door, aware that if my mom wants to eavesdrop, she'll find a way to do it, door in her way or not.

"I love your mom."

Finally, I let my laughter out. "She's one of a kind, that's for sure."

The humor dies quickly. "What the hell was that? With Ann?" Isabelle voices the question plaguing me since I saw Ann in the doorway.

"I have no idea."

"Finn, I swear, if I thought she'd show up here, I never would have said you had family visiting."

When she hangs her head, I rush to her side and pull her into my arms. "Izzy, don't. This isn't your fault. Not one bit of it."

"It is. I should have insisted you go to her house last night and I could've stayed with your mom. Maybe then she'd have backed off."

"Izzy, look at me." I tip her chin up. "Ann is unstable and unfortunately, we're learning just how unpredictable she is." I shrug. "I don't like that she's figured out where I live but it's done. And it's not your fault."

"Listen to my boy, Isabelle," my mom yells through the door. "He's smart, my Finnigan."

Again, Isabelle and I exchange glances and this time, we both break out into laughter. Happy that Isabelle's mood has lightened, I remind myself to thank my mother later for being so nosy.

"Let's go eat," I suggest and tug her toward the door. "I'll text Isaiah really quick and ask him to call a meeting tomorrow so we can figure out our next steps."

"You don't need to text him. I'll send out a mass text and call the meeting myself."

"I grin. "Okay."

She rises to her tiptoes and kisses me on the cheek.

"What was that for?" I ask.

"For not arguing. For trusting me." Her smile widens. "For being you."

25

## ISABELLE

"Quiet down." Isaiah bangs the table to get everyone's attention. When he's met with silence, he looks at me. "Isabelle called this meeting so let's give her all of our focus."

I rise from my chair and walk to the head of the table to stand next to him. This is the first time I've been handed the reins to run the meeting and I hate to admit it, but I'm nervous. I've grown up around these people, built my life around the club and what we do, and I'm still not sure how they'll react to what I have to say.

"Thanks for coming on such short notice. I appreciate it." I allow my eyes to drift toward Finn and my nerves jump up a notch. I haven't talked to him about this, but I have talked to Isaiah. This is either a good call or it will blow up in my face. "Before we get down to business with our case, I'd like to put Finn Walsh's club membership to a vote."

Finn's eyes widen and I worry that this is going the wrong way. When his features relax, so do I.

"Isabelle is the one putting this to a vote," Isaiah says from beside me. "But I want you all to know that I support this one hundred percent. Finn has been invaluable to our most recent case, but he's also proven to be loyal, honorable, and invested in this club and what we stand for."

"We don't have all voting members present," Jace reminds us.

"Cooper and Lila are with Finn's mother at his place for reasons you'll understand later. They both gave me their votes before they left."

"Those in favor of making Finn a permanent patched member, raise your hands," Liam instructs.

Shock settles into my gut at the response. Every hand goes up. I expected that. What I didn't expect was for Finn's hand to also be up.

"Brother, you do know you don't get a vote in this, right?" Isaiah jokes.

"I do know that," Finn replies with a laugh. "But I wanted you to see how I feel about it. I've given you some shit. I've had a fucking attitude from hell and fought you every step of the way. At least in the beginning. But now?" He pauses and locks eyes with me. "Now, I'm home. I've found where I belong. I've found my people."

My heart skips a beat as Isaiah bends down to get the cut from under the table and walks it to Finn. It skips another when Finn puts it on.

"Welcome to the family."

Isaiah pulls Finn in for a bear hug and cheers reverberate around the room. I take it all in, enjoy the moment, because I know when I start talking again, the happiness will die, at least temporarily.

When I can no longer put it off, I pound my fist on the table to get everyone's attention. All chatter stops and all eyes turn to me.

"I know that this should be a time to celebrate. And I promise you, we will celebrate our newest member. But right now, we have a problem that we need to address, and I need you all to focus."

"Before Isabelle jumps in, does anyone need a refresher on the Ann Brindle case?" Liam asks.

"She's the lady from the bar, right? The one with the psycho ex and his douchebag friends?"

"That's her."

"No, we're all good."

I spend the next hour giving an update, providing all of the details of the last few days, starting with Ann's trip to the ER and ending with her appearance at Finn's place. The longer I talk, the angrier the faces around the table become.

"I did a deeper dive into Carson," Liam says. "And I gotta say, I'm starting to doubt his guilt in a lot of things. When we took the case, Ann handed us court orders, custody orders, police reports. She handed over all of the documentation we needed to get started and, at the time, we took it at face value." He sighs. "We shouldn't have."

"What have you found?" I ask.

"For starters, her documentation was all fake."

"All of it?" Finn demands.

Liam shakes his head. "No, not all. But ninety-nine percent of it. The only thing in there that seems to be on the up and up is the court order granting Ann full custody of their son."

"Were you able to determine why Carson wasn't even given shared custody?"

"Carson isn't innocent by any means. He's had numerous DUI arrests, one of which occurred when he was transporting his son. The judge that got the case is particularly hard on parents who drive drunk with a kid in the car. Ann knew that and on the advice of her attorney, she filed for custody within twenty-four hours of that incident. She won."

"And there are no official reports of domestic violence or abuse?"

"Oh, there are reports," Liam counters. "I'm just not sure how truthful Ann was being when she made them."

"So what is our theory on this? Ann is a liar and doesn't need our help or Ann is a liar but coincidentally is also in danger from someone other than her ex? Those are two very different things."

"My theory is a combination of both," I reply. "Liam, show them what you were able to dig up in her medical history."

Liam pulls out copies of documentation and passes them around the table. "Ann hasn't had the easiest life. She was passed around from foster home to foster home. She also has twelve admissions into different psych wards across the country for self-harm incidents."

"Okay, so she has mental problems. But she didn't make up Carson's buddies at the bar. We were all there."

"I think that was staged."

Skeptical glances are aimed at me and I hold my hand up to stop any protests. "I know that sounds nuts, and it goes against everything we stand for to doubt the victim. But my gut says that Carson isn't an issue and those weren't his friends."

"What about the time he showed up at group?" Tillie asks, clearly unconvinced. "That behavior doesn't strike me as unthreatening."

"I agree. But Finn and I have rehashed that scene a dozen times and we keep coming back to the fact that he was simply angry because Ann's been denying him access to their son. She has full custody, but he does have visitation. The last time he saw the boy was months ago."

"Okay, I can get on board with that. But flat-out calling Ann a liar? I don't know," Ruby says.

"Tell them about the cigarette butts, Iz," my brother says.

I explain the pile I found outside of Ann's window. "Isaiah pulled strings with a tech at the forensic lab and had one of the butts DNA tested."

"And?" Ruby prods.

"It came back as a match to Ann."

"That makes no sense."

"The pile was under some windows on the side of her house. One of those windows was in Ann's bedroom. My guess is she's a closet smoker and tosses the butts out the window when she's done."

"So she's a closet smoker. A lot of people are."

"True, but most people wouldn't lie to me about it when they know I'm testing it as a means to prove who was standing outside her window. Not only that but she had to know the DNA would come back to her." I look at Finn and nod for him to take his turn.

"For some reason, Ann has set her sights on me. I don't know why, other than I was the first person to check on her at the bar. Apparently, that's all that matters."

"Aw, you've got a fan."

"A fan I don't want," Finn retorts. "Ann is dangerous. And I want her dealt with."

"As do we," Isaiah assures him.

"Wait," Liam says, a serious look on his face. "Go back a minute. If we're running with our theory about Ann and all of her fear and injuries and whatever is bullshit, then what are we saying about Iz's shooting? Someone shot her."

"I think it was Ann," Finn says and a hush falls around the room.

"Calling a woman crazy is one thing, pinning attempted murder on her is something altogether different."

"True. But I don't think her aim was to kill Izzy," Finn explains. "Izzy was shot at close range. If Ann wanted her dead, she'd have hit a major organ, at the very least. Instead, the bullet tore through skin and not much else."

"Felt like a lot more than that," I grumble.

"I know it did. But think about it," Finn insists. "It's the only thing that makes sense. Unless we want to subscribe to the theory that Isabelle's shooting is something completely unrelated. I'm not saying that's not possible, but it's highly unlikely."

"Listen, we're not asking you to completely change your way of thinking. We're simply asking you to trust us, trust our guts, and trust that we wouldn't have brought this to the table if we really didn't believe what we're telling you."

"Okay, fine. We go with you on this. What's the plan?"

"That's why we need all of you," I say. "We don't have a plan. We're hoping that, together, we can come up with something."

Before anyone can say anything, a cell phone dings.

"Dammit! No phones during meetings," Isaiah barks.

"It's mine," Finn says apologetically. "I left it on in case my mother needed anything."

"Is everything okay?" Isaiah asks.

Finn looks at his phone and the color drains from his face.

"Finn, brother, what's up?" Liam asks.

Finn lunges toward the door and I rush after him. The other members follow.

"Finn, talk to us. What happened?" I shout at his back.

Without stopping, without even slowing down, he yells over his shoulder.

"Stupid bitch has my mother."

# 26

# FINN

*W*ind smacks me in the face as I break every speed limit to get to my house. I repeat a litany of reassurances in my head, over and over again, trying to convince myself that the picture I saw on my cell, the one of my mother tied to a chair with blood trickling down her cheek, is somehow fake. That it's all one big practical joke or a nightmare I'll wake up from.

How did this happen? How did Ann get past Cooper and Lila? What the fuck was I thinking, leaving my mother to go play biker detective with the Brotherhood? I have no answers and honestly, I'm not sure I want them. Because I'm afraid they'll all point back to me being a selfish prick who doesn't put other's safety above my own needs.

When I reach my driveway, I pull in and lay my bike down, not giving a damn if it gets dented or scratched. It can be fixed. If my mother is dead, there's no fixing that. I race up the steps and burst through the front door, fully expecting to see a gruesome scene. That's not even close to the reality in front of me.

There doesn't appear to be anything out of place. There

are no signs of a struggle and there would've had to have been for Ann to have gotten past Cooper and Lila. There are no drops of blood on the floor, no broken glass or rumpled furniture. There's nothing. I methodically make my way through the house, only slowing down enough to grab my gun out of the safe in my bedroom, and still, I find nothing.

"Mom!" I shout into the silence.

And silence is exactly what greets me. As I retreat from the bedroom and head to the kitchen, my mind races.

*Think Finn! Where the fuck could they be?*

The only place left to check is the basement. I keep the door leading down locked so I doubt I'll find anything, but I can't take any chances. In the kitchen, I'm greeted with much of the same: nothing. There's a skillet in the dishrack and a quick glance tells me that it's still not quite dry. That's odd.

When I turn to the basement door, my stomach falls. The lock is busted, and the door is cracked open. I take a deep breath and try to brace myself for what I'm going to find but a noise behind me pulls my attention.

I whirl around, gun drawn, and see Isaiah and Isabelle standing there, weapons in hand.

"I could have fucking shot you," I snarl. "Don't sneak up on a person."

"Brother, we called your name... twice," Isaiah says. "There was no sneaking."

That makes sense. In the military, I was always told that I was intense. That, no matter the mission, no matter the chaos around me, I'd zone out, focus completely on the task at hand. I've always thought that made me a better soldier but if it's what caused me to almost shoot Isabelle, it's a problem.

"I don't think anyone is here, but I still need to check the basement."

Isabelle's face twists with concern. "Why don't you let us go check?"

"I can handle whatever we find," I snap, not giving a damn if I hurt her feelings. "Either stay behind me or stay up here."

Without letting another minute pass, I turn and walk down the steps, swinging my gun back and forth as I go so I don't miss any opportunity that may present itself to shoot. The basement is quiet, dark, eerie. It doesn't feel anything like the place that typically brings me comfort, offers me an escape from the world.

When I hit the bottom step, something catches my eye in the far corner. I rush forward, ignoring the pain in my stump, and that's when I see them. Cooper and Lila are in the corner, rope securing their arms and legs, duct tape covering their mouths.

Cooper is writhing, no doubt trying to get free, and Lila is doing much of the same. Isaiah and I work to free them and once they are, they both stand. Lila curls into Cooper and he holds onto her as if she could disappear at any moment.

"What the fuck happened?" I demand. "How did she get in the house? How the hell did you let her get my—"

The breath is knocked out of me when my back hit's the cement wall. Cooper is holding me against it with his hands fisted in my shirt and he's as close to my face as he can get.

"Don't you ever accuse me of allowing something like this to happen, got it?" I glare at him but don't respond. "I don't know how Ann got in the house. I'd secured it no more than thirty minutes before everything went down. Locks, windows, doors... everything was in place, sealed up tight. The next thing I know, your mom is falling to the floor and Lila and I are hit with a fucking taser."

I struggle against Cooper as he talks but my fight dies when he mentions my mom.

"Where did she take my mom?"

Lila rests her hand on my arm. "We don't know. Finn," she shakes her head. "Jesus, Finn, we couldn't do anything. As soon as she tased us, she dragged us down here and tied us up. It wasn't too long after that that we heard her leave."

"Well, she took my mother with her. There's nothing upstairs."

"Hey, guys," Isabelle calls. "I found the taser."

We all make our way to Isabelle.

"Motherfucker!" I rasp out, yanking it from Isabelle's hands.

Isaiah starts barking instructions. "Iz, call Doc and tell him what we've got. See if this is something that Cooper and Lila need medical attention for. I'm—"

"We're fine, Pres," Cooper insists.

"No arguments," Isaiah snarls. "We're not taking any chances." He returns to his orders. "I'm gonna call Liam and see if he found anything in his research that would tell us where they went. Finn, you keep calling your mother's cell. I know she likely won't answer but hopefully with the incoming calls, Liam or Griffin can work their magic and trace a location."

"What about her house?" I ask because that seems the likely place.

"I don't think she's that stupid. I sent guys there anyway, just to be sure. I expect to hear from them soon."

As Isaiah and Isabelle make their calls, I pace, taking my frustration and fear out on the punching bag each time I pass it. Cooper and Lila sit on the bench, having been given no instructions on what to do, and while a part of me wants to rage at them, demand they do something, I don't. This isn't their fault.

Isabelle steps in my path and flattens her hands on my

chest. "We're going to find her, Finn. We're going to find her and she's going to be fine. I promise."

"You don't know that," I bark.

"Yeah, I do. It's what we do. It's what we're good at. Believe in that. Believe in *us*."

"What did Doc say?" Cooper asks from behind us.

"He said you should be fine. He'll check you both over when you get home but no need to go to the hospital."

"You both need to head back to the main house," Isaiah says as he steps up next to us. "We can handle everything from here. I don't want you to wait to have Doc check you out. It'd be our luck that we'd wait and then a problem would arise."

Cooper and Lila both start protesting but Isaiah holds up his hands to silence them. "Enough. Do what you're told."

Cooper's jaw clenches and Lila balls her hands into fists at her sides. They are clearly not happy with Isaiah but rather than argue further, they do as they're told. When they reach the top of the steps, Cooper stops and stoops down to look at us.

"Call us as soon as you find her."

I give a curt nod, not trusting myself to speak. They disappear upstairs and it isn't long before I hear the familiar rumble of a Harley. Funny, I don't remember seeing it when I pulled into the driveway but then again, my mind was on other things.

"We need to head out," Isaiah says, capturing my attention. He starts up the stairs, talking to us over his shoulder. "Liam is texting me a location. Fortunately, he had the foresight to install an app on your mom's phone when you all were at the main house for dinner. Sort of like the 'Find My Phone' app."

"What the fuck? Why hasn't he been able to give us a location yet?"

"Because, your mom's phone hasn't stayed within range of a cell tower, making it hard to pinpoint an exact location."

Just then, my cell phone pings with a text. Thinking it's Liam with a location, I don't check the number before swiping to read it.

**You're taking too long. I'm not sure how much time mommy dearest has left.**

My blood runs cold, yet it feels like my veins are burning a path through my body.

*Please don't die. I'll find you, Mom. Just hang on.*

Isabelle's small hand rests on my lower back but I pull away from her and head upstairs. I can hear them on the steps behind me, but it doesn't slow me down. I storm through the house, out the front door to my Harley.

"Where are you going?" Isabelle calls out to me as I lift the bike up.

"To find them," I snap as I straddle the metal beast.

"Finn, stop." Isaiah's tone is firm, demanding, authoritative. I ignore him. "Dammit, Finn, I said stop."

Isaiah grabs my arm and yanks on me, almost causing me to topple over. "Where the fuck are you gonna go? Huh? We have no clue yet where they are. You can't just take off and drive around, willy-nilly. That doesn't do anyone a fucking bit of good."

I shake him off of me. "I can do whatever the hell I want. I'm not going to sit here with my thumb up my ass and do nothing!"

"Finn, please," Isabelle pleads from next to her brother. "Stop and think this through. Isaiah is right. You know he's—"

My phone rings, cutting her off. I glance at the screen, praying to see my mother's number and tensing when I don't recognize the number. My eyes dart to Isaiah and Isabelle and back to my phone.

"Answer it," Isaiah demands.

I hit the button to accept the call and slowly lift the cell to my ear. "Where is she?"

"Is this Finn Walsh?" A voice asks.

"Who the fuck is this?"

"I'm a deputy and I've got an inmate who insists on speaking to you." He pauses. "Do you know a Carson Brindle?"

My eyes widen and I nod before remembering that he can't see me. "Yes. Put him on the phone."

A rustling noise comes through the line, as if he's handing the phone over and while I wait for Carson, I hit the speaker-phone button so that Isaiah and Isabelle can hear.

"I know where they are," Carson says the minute he has the phone.

"I swear on all that's holy, if you have anything to do with this, I will kill you."

"I don't. But I got a call from Ann early this morning. I've been trying to convince someone to let me call you and they finally did."

"Where are they?" I ask, not giving a shit about his issues in jail.

"Early in our marriage, Ann and I liked to get away some-times. We owned a cabin near Nashville."

"Tennessee?"

"No, Indiana. It's a bit south. Anyway, she got the cabin in the divorce. I gave in on that because I was hoping she'd give a little on the custody issue if she got everything else she wanted."

"I need an address."

Carson rattles off an address but also provides directions because apparently, the cabin is 'hard to find'. "There are a lot of weapons at the cabin, assuming she's kept them," Carson adds. "I like to hunt so there are several rifles and a lot of knives and tools to skin deer, butcher them. There's..." He takes a deep breath. "Just be careful. Ann is dang—"

I end the call, not wanting to hear about Ann and how dangerous she is. I already know. I shove my cell in my pocket and rev the engine of my bike. Isaiah goes to his own Harley and Isabelle straddles mine behind me.

"What are you doing?" I ask.

"I'm riding with you."

"I'm not going to go slow. I'm not going to take it easy just so you can hang on."

"Wouldn't expect you to."

I nod and circle my arm in the air.

"Let's ride!"

# 27

# ISABELLE

*E*very few minutes, Finn rests his hand on my thigh and digs his fingers in, almost as if he's reassuring himself that I'm still here. My arms are linked around his waist and I'm holding on as tight as I can, but I don't think it's registering with him. His mind is far ahead of us, at the cabin, and no doubt it's playing out every awful scenario we may find.

My mind races, my heartbeat roars in my ears. How did we miss this? Were there signs that we should have seen earlier? I don't have the answers and I'm afraid no one ever will.

After almost an hour of frantic travel, I start to see landmarks and signs that Carson told us to watch for.

"We're almost there," I shout, hoping Finn hears me.

When we reach the road that Carson told us the cabin is on, Finn pulls off to the side and cuts the engine. Isaiah pulls up behind us.

"Why are we stopping?" Isaiah asks.

"She'll hear the bikes. I don't want her to have a heads up that we're coming."

Isaiah nods as he looks up and down the road. "Carson said the cabin was what? Half a mile or so in that direction?" He points straight ahead.

"Something like that." Finn takes off walking.

Isaiah and I exchange glances and then Isaiah says, "I don't suppose there's any reason to believe you'd listen to me if I told you to stay put?"

"Not a single reason," I assure him and start jogging to catch up to Finn.

Isaiah falls into step beside us, and we trudge forward like the three musketeers on a mission. It doesn't take long to reach the edge of the property line, marked by an iron cross sticking out of the ground, just like Carson said.

Isaiah grabs Finn's arm and stops him. "What's your plan?"

"Go in, get my mother, get out," Finn responds as if it's going to be just that simple.

I wish he were right. I wish we could charge in there and grab Margaret and leave. But that's not how this will go down and I feel like I need to remind Finn of that, before he gets himself, or someone else, killed.

"Finn, we need a plan. You know as well as I do that this isn't a quick snatch and grab deal. Carson said that Ann has access to a lot of weapons and the bitch is unstable. We. Need. A. Plan."

"What do you suggest? We knock on the door and hope she invites us in for fucking tea?!"

"Actually, that might work," Isaiah says, causing Finn and I to shift and look at him, Finn poised to argue.

"Let me explain," he rushes before Finn can get a word out. "Ann has set her sights on you, right?" Finn nods. "If we barge in there, she's gonna be on the defensive. But if you go in alone, play into her hand, there's a better chance that you can talk her down, hopefully resulting in no further injuries."

"If I go in alone, where will you and Isabelle be?"

"You won't be completely alone. We'll be at the back, watching, ready to come in if we need to."

"Izzy, what do you think?" Finn asks me.

"I think it's the best option."

"Okay." Finn pulls me toward him and presses his lips to mine. The kiss is hard, demanding, and over before it really begins. "Be careful. I love you."

Before I can respond, he takes off ahead of my brother and me, his shoulders squared, his head held high. I watch as he tucks his gun into the back of his waistband and I want to tell him to keep it ready, just in case.

"He'll be fine, Iz."

"He better be."

Isaiah grips my arm and pulls me with him toward the tree line. We'll make our way through the pines and to the back of the house. To my surprise, and delight, there are several windows that allow us to see through the cabin and into the living area.

Isaiah and I crouch down below the sill so we can't be seen. Voices carry and we're able to hear everything going on, which is also a nice surprise. I hear Ann talking to Margaret. Nothing important, mostly rambling about how she's sorry she had to hurt her but that it'll be over soon, and they'll be 'one big happy family'. Margaret isn't responding.

I stand up and look through the window. Margaret is tied to a chair, but she appears conscious. I can't see her face, so I don't know if she's still bleeding but Ann better pray that she's not. Ann is pacing back and forth, a rifle in her hand.

Suddenly, Ann rushes to the door and pulls it open. I see as she launches herself into Finn's arms. He catches her easily, but his face is a mask of disgust. He'll do what he has to do but he's not going to like a single second of it.

"I knew you'd come," Ann says, and Finn sets her on her feet.

"I came." His eyes dart from Ann to his mother. "Mom, are you okay?"

"I'm fine, Finnigan. Happy you're here."

"Good. That's good."

"Finn, I didn't hurt her. I would never hurt Mom."

*Her delusions know no bounds.*

I glance at Isaiah and roll my eyes. He glares at me and I force myself to sober. There's nothing funny about the situation, I know that, but it's hard to keep a straight face with all the crazy spewing from Ann's mouth.

"I believe you, Ann," Finn says, his tone flat and even. He takes a step forward and reaches for the rifle. "Why don't you let me take that? That way, no one gets hurt."

Ann bolts away from him. "No!" She wraps both arms around the gun. "No, you're not taking it. It's mine. I need it."

Finn raises both hands. "You can keep it, Ann. I'm sorry." He steps toward his mother. "I'm just going to check and make sure she's okay."

Ann doesn't stop him, but she watches him closely. Finn leans down and speaks to his mother, but it's so quiet I can't hear, and I can't even attempt to read his lips because Margaret is blocking my view.

"This is taking too long," Isaiah mumbles.

"No kidding."

"Ann, what do you want from me?" I hear Finn ask.

"I want you to love me," she cries. "I know you can. You already have feelings for me. You were worried about me, that night at the bar. You have feelings for me, Finn, I know it."

Finn's muscles bunch as he shifts his weight. He thrusts a hand through his hair, no doubt trying to figure out what to say. The problem is it doesn't matter what he says.

"Finnigan, I think Ann would make a lovely addition to the family," Margaret says calmly.

"See," Ann yells. "Your mom loves me already. We're off to a great start."

Finn's jaw tics. "Yeah, we are."

"Ann, would you mind if Finnigan untied me? I'd really like to use the restroom?"

Ann looks from Margaret to Finn and back again. She lifts the rifle and points it at Finn. "Go ahead, but don't try anything stupid."

Finn rushes to untie Margaret. When her wrists and ankles are free, he helps her stand. She wobbles slightly but manages to steady herself by leaning on her son.

"The bathroom's over there." Ann points toward a hall. "First door."

Finn guides his mother in the direction Ann indicated and that's when everything goes from bad to worse. I don't know if Margaret sees Isaiah and me or just senses our presence, but she pauses for a split-second and Ann picks up on the shit.

Isaiah and I flatten ourselves to the logs, under the window, and hold our breath. I can hear Ann stomping close. I hear the tap of the rifle barrel on the glass. And then I hear her shout.

"What the hell are they doing here, Finn?"

Shit!

"What are you talking about?" Finn asks. "Who?"

"Those people," she screams. "Those... those home-wreckers!"

Making a snap decision, I stand up and move to my left where the back door is. I twist the knob and find it unlocked and step inside, my hands raised. I don't look at Margaret or Finn. I focus all of my attention on Ann.

"Finn didn't know we were here."

Ann points the rifle at me. "I don't believe you."

"He didn't," Isaiah assures her as he steps next to me.

"Then why are you here?"

"We figured out that you were lying to us. When we heard that you took Finn's mom and that he came here to be with you, we rushed here to stop him." The words are like acid on my tongue. Bile rises up the back of my throat, but I swallow it down. "I love Finn and I couldn't wrap my head around the fact that he doesn't love me, that he wants you instead."

Ann lowers the gun and turns to Finn. "Is that true?"

"Yes."

"I'm sorry to interrupt, but I still need to use the restroom," Margaret says.

"Oh, Mom," Ann cries as she rushes forward. "Here, let me help you."

Finn tries to stop her, but Margaret shakes her head. "I'll be fine, Finnigan. Why don't you show Isabelle and Isaiah out?"

"I want them gone when we get back," Ann adds in a sing-song voice.

The three of us watch as Ann and Margaret disappear down the hall and behind the bathroom door. I don't even try to make sense of the fact that Ann goes in with Margaret or why she feels comfortable leaving the three of us out here alone. There's no reason to try because it doesn't make sense.

"We can't leave," I insist.

"You might have to," Finn says. "I don't know how else to keep her flip from switching into full blown psycho mode."

"What if we go out the front and sneak back around to where we were?" I ask. "She won't be expecting that."

"I wouldn't be so sure," Finn argues. "She's nuts, so there's no telling what we can get past her."

"Is that what you really think?"

We turn toward Ann, who's standing just at the end of the

hallway, and I notice that she no longer has the rifle. She shoves Margaret forward and Finn's mother stumbles but doesn't fall.

"Do you really think I'm nuts?" Ann asks again.

"No, of course not," Finn pushes out in an effort to reassure her.

"If you think I'll believe you, apparently you also think I'm stupid."

"Ann," Margaret begins and turns around to face her. "No one thinks th—"

The gunshot startles a scream from me and, as if in slow motion, Margaret crumples to the floor. Finn rushes forward but Ann points the pistol at him. Where the hell did she get the pistol?

"Don't," Ann barks. "It's better this way. Mom was only going to get in our way, Finn. We wouldn't have been happy with her in the picture."

My eyes never leave Margaret. Blood seeps from a hole in her stomach and I know if she has any chance of surviving, she needs medical attention fast. A quick glance at Ann assures me that she's focused on Finn. No longer caring what she does or how reckless it might be, I drop to my knees and press my hands to Margaret's wound.

"C'mon, Margaret," I plead. "Hang in there for me."

"Step away from her," Ann demands, her voice eerily calm.

"No."

I hear Finn and Isaiah moving, closing in on Ann. They won't be able to stop her. As long as she's waving a pistol around and pulling the trigger like it's nothing, she's got a leg up on them.

A gunshot reverberates through the cabin and I hear glass shatter. "Get out!" Ann shouts. "All of you, get the hell out of my house!"

I glare at her. "If I leave, I'm taking Margaret with me."

A light touch on my hand pulls my attention away from Ann. Margaret is awake and her lips are moving. I lean over her, placing my ear close to her mouth to try and make sense of her words.

"Take..." Margaret coughs and moans. "Take care of my Finnigan."

"I'll take care of your son," Ann barks. "Not her."

"Please, Isa—"

Pain like I've never felt before explodes in my chest and that sensation is the last thing I remember before the world around me goes black.

# FINN

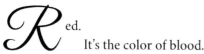ed.
 It's the color of blood.

Red.

It means stop.

Red.

It's the color of fire.

Red.

It's a burning rage that is all consuming, the haze the clouds my vision, the beast that bursts from me and lunges at Ann. I'm dimly aware of Isaiah, dropping to his knees and tending to Isabelle and my mom. Beyond that, my sole focus is on the woman who, in minutes, burned my world to the ground for the second time in as many years.

Ann and I tumble to the ground, wrestling over the gun. She manages to hit me in the head with the butt of it, which stuns me long enough for her to get up and try to run. I pull my own weapon out of my waistband, cock it, aim at the ceiling, and pull the trigger.

"Stop!" I shout at her.

Ann stops but when she turns around and raises the gun,

I watch her trigger finger. The slightest twitch and I'll end her.

"We would have been happy," she cries. "I could have made you very happy."

"No, Ann, you couldn't."

Her finger shifts and I pull the trigger. Ann drops to the floor, blood flowing from the hole in her forehead, her eyes staring sightlessly. I shift gears and drop down next to Isaiah.

I lift Isabelle's head into my lap. "C'mon, baby, open those eyes for me." I rock her back and forth, silently begging her to live.

"Ambulance is on the way," Isaiah says, his hands pressing the wound on my mother's stomach. "Should be here any minute."

"I can't lose them, Isaiah." My eyes burn and I blink several times to stop the tears from falling. "I can't. I've lost so much, and I won't survive losing them."

"Stop!" Isaiah barks. "Stop talking. You aren't going to lose them. *We* aren't going to lose them."

The sound of sirens reaches my ears and I experience the first flutter of hope I've felt all day. The closer the ambulance gets, the louder the sirens.

In a matter of minutes, the cabin is full of EMTs and police. Liam also arrives with Cooper, Griffin, and Micah. I'm pulled away from Isabelle and I strain against the arms around me.

"Let them do their job, Son."

I glare at Griffin. "I can't lose them."

"You're not losing anyone."

Isabelle and my mom are loaded onto gurneys and rushed outside to the two waiting ambulances. Micah and Isaiah follow, I assume to ride with Isabelle. Griffin drags me outside and pushes me toward the rig my mom is in.

"Go. We'll meet you all there."

"But wh—"

"Go!"

I hop in the back and the doors close. The ride to the hospital is tense, bumpy, and far too long. I hold my mom's hand and I pray. I haven't prayed since before the bombing but I'm praying now. Praying, bargaining, pleading with whatever higher power is out there to keep them alive.

The driver slams on the breaks and that's when I realize we've made it. A flurry of activity surrounds me. My mom is taken inside and when I jump down to the ground, I see doctor's rushing Isabelle inside as well.

Isaiah and Micah hop down from the other ambulance. Micah runs inside but Isaiah stops next to me. The two of us, we stand there in silence for a few minutes, neither one of us quite sure what to say.

Isaiah is finally the one to break the silence. "You should have a doctor look at your stump. Today had to have been rough on it."

I nod but don't move.

"Finn?"

I put one foot in front of the other and move. It's difficult, it's painful, but I do it. I'm whisked to a curtained room by a nurse who takes my vitals and hands me a gown.

"Sir, please put this on."

On autopilot, I start to take off my clothes. Before I drop my pants, the nurse leaves, muttering something indistinguishable. I put the gown on, hop up on the table, and as I loosen my prosthesis and it falls to the floor, Emersyn walks in.

"I can see you're not gonna be any different than the rest of them," she quips while she reads a chart.

"Have you seen my mom? Isabelle? How are they?"

She looks at me with sympathy. "They're in surgery."

I become a little more aware of my surroundings. "They're alive?"

Emersyn smiles. "They are."

"And they're gonna make it?"

She turns away from me and grabs supplies from a cabinet. Emersyn takes her time doing whatever the hell it is that she's doing, and my concern grows.

"Emersyn, answer me."

When she returns her stare to me, her face falls. "I don't know, Finn." She sits on a rolling stool in front of me and starts cleaning my stump and putting a cream on it. "This should help with some of the chafing. I'm also going to give you something to help settle your nerves that should minimize the pain as well."

"Fine, great." I push her hands away from my leg, causing her to look up. "Why don't you know if they'll make it?"

She takes deep breaths as she stands to fill a syringe, presumably with whatever medicine she just told me about. As she injects it into my arm, she answers my question. "Your mother lost a lot of blood. The bullet missed all the major organs, which is good, but they're still trying to remove it. It's dangerously close to her spine."

"Izzy?"

Emersyn's eyes well up with tears. "Iz's injury is a bit more complicated."

I try to get off the table and Emersyn pushes me back.

"I need to see them," I groan.

"And you will, after surgery."

"Why is Izzy's injury more complicated?"

"The bullet struck her ribs, shattering two and sending pieces of bone to puncture her lung. She's coded twice already. They're doing everything they can to keep her alive and patch her up but…"

"But it might not work," I finish for her.

"It might not."

"Does everyone else know?" I ask, thinking of Isaiah and Micah and all the Brotherhood members who have known Isabelle her entire life.

"The doctor is with them now, filling them is."

I nod absently.

"Finn, do you have any other family I should be calling?"

I shake my head. "My mom is my only family." I glance toward the door. "And them. My mom and the Brotherhood are all I've got."

She rests a hand on my arm. "Okay. Take your time getting dressed and then you can head on out to the waiting room with everyone else. As for your stump, put this on it every few hours." She hands me a tube of cream.

"Thanks Emersyn."

She smiles and then walks through the curtain, leaving me alone. I lay back on the table and try to gather my thoughts. I still feel like I'm in a hazy fog but I'm not sure I want to escape it. In the fog, there's still hope that things on the outside will get better. If I escape now, I have to face reality. A reality in which my mother and the love of my life don't make it.

I like the fog.

~

"Finn."

The weight on my eyelids is heavy. So very heavy.

"Finn, wake up."

I roll to my side and try to block out the voice.

"Finnigan Walsh!"

I shoot into a sitting position and when I see Isaiah standing there, Liam next to him, I get off the table and reach for my prosthesis. The events of the day slam into me. The memory, along with the looks on their faces has my heart cracking and my knee buckles just before I collapse on the floor.

"No." The words tear out of me, guttural and full of pain. "No, no, no, no."

Isaiah rushes forward and wraps his arm around me. Liam joins him and they both make every effort to get me up but fail. They're talking to me, saying words that don't make sense. Or maybe they do. I can't hear anything specific over my wails.

"No, no, no, no, no, no."

The world starts to close in on me. Maybe it's my brain's way of protecting me from the pain or maybe my body is finally shutting down because it realizes there's no reason to hold on anymore. Either way, as the blackness engulfs me, I welcome it.

Isabelle and my mother are there to greet me, just beyond a bright light. Their arms are outstretched, waiting, welcoming. Neither of them show signs of the trauma that killed them and I'm grateful that they don't have to live with their wounds for all eternity.

I run toward them and realize that it feels... different. I look down and see that I have both legs. Apparently, all wounds are healed in the ever after. I pick up my pace, laughing as I run, but then it hits me. The longer I run, the further away they get.

"Wait for me," I call to them.

I force my legs to pump harder, faster, but it makes no difference. They're still getting farther and farther away.

"Finn, c'mon," Isabelle says with her arm out. "You can do it."

"I'm trying," I shout.

Suddenly, the light disappears and is replaced by a black hole. My leg disappears and I fall to the ground, confused, scared, in pain. I stare at the hole in front of me, try to command it with my mind to be the light again, to give me Isabelle and my mother back.

"Finn, I love you."

No, that can't be right. Isabelle is still there, in that darkness? She doesn't belong there.

I writhe on the ground. I scream, I shout, I yell out to the universe that they got it wrong. That Isabelle is too good to be in Hell.

A cold sensation spreads through my arm. I look at it and see my veins moving, slithering under my skin as if the cold is dragging them around. I flatten my hand over them, trying to make them stop and feel another hand settle on top of mine.

I look around and see no one. I'm alone, but I'm not. Who is touching me?

"Finn?" I reach toward the voice. "Dammit, Finn, open your eyes."

Light starts to seep through the darkness. My hand connects with something solid and then something soft. What the hell? The light continues to brighten as the darkness fades and shapes appear before me.

"Damn, Brother, you scared us."

My brow creases and I roll my neck to see Isaiah grinning at me. "No, this isn't right. You're not dead. You didn't die."

"No shit," he counters. "Neither did you. You passed out from shock."

"But I saw Izzy, my mom, they—"

"I'm right here."

I roll over quickly but all I see is the rails of the hospital bed I'm lying in and the rails of another one next to it. I glance back at Isaiah and he's stifling a laugh.

"What the hell is so funny?"

"If you could see the look on your face you wouldn't have

to ask." He walks around the bed and reaches into the other bed, lifting up a small hand. "Iz didn't die. She's right here."

I sit up slowly, my eyes glued to the bed, and there she is. Hooked up to an IV and bandaged, but alive. Isabelle is alive.

I glare at Isaiah. "Why the fuck did you let me think she died?"

"Liam and I tried to tell you," he insists. "You were in shock, man. Nothing we said was sinking in."

"And my mom?" I ask, hating that it's almost an afterthought.

"She's made it through surgery and is in the ICU. The doctors were just waiting for you to wake up to take you to see her."

"Why is she in the ICU?"

"The amount of blood loss, the length of the surgery, her age... they just want to be sure she's monitored extra closely."

"You can thank our dad for that," Isabelle says from her bed. "Emersyn will be working the ICU floor the next few days, so we wanted to be sure she'd be the one taking care of your mom."

"Okay." I rub my forehead, trying to process it all. "I appreciate that."

"You're family. It's what we do."

I chuckle. "Right."

"I'll leave you two alone for a minute," Isaiah says. "The doctors will be back soon to take Iz back to her room. They only brought her in here because they were hoping she'd be able to help wake you up."

"Thanks, brother."

Isaiah leaves and I take my time getting out of bed. I pull the IV out of my hand, the one that I assume was pumping fluids into me. That explains the cold sensation I felt. I step up to Isabelle's bed and look at her, grateful that she's there to look at.

"Are you just gonna stand there and stare?"

"Maybe, just for a minute."

"Finn, I'm so sorry you got caught up in all of this."

I lean over and press a kiss to her lips. "Hush," I whisper against them. "If you'll remember, I jumped into the fight at the bar. I got myself into it all on my own."

"You should probably go see your mom."

"Marry me."

The words are out of my mouth before I even stop to think them through. I realize it doesn't matter though. I'd have said them whether I had a minute to think them through or a year to think them through. But judging by Isabelle's silence, I may be the only one that wants this.

"Forget it," I push out. "I can see—"

"Why do you want to marry me?" she asks.

"Because I love you. Because when I thought I'd lost you today, I didn't want to live. Look, I know that we haven't known each other that long and some people might think we're crazy, but I don't care. If I've learned anything in life, it's that tomorrow isn't promised. So when you find a person you want to spend your life with, you do that, you spend your life with them. Whether that's another ten days or ten years or ten decades. I want that with you, Izzy. I love you. I didn't want to. You didn't fit in with my bitter hold on the past, but you pulled me out of it. You're the only person who could." I pause and take a deep breath. "And did I mention that I love you?"

"Yes."

"I thought so, but it bears repeating."

"No." She shakes her head. "I mean, yes you told me you loved me. But I also mean, yes, I'll marry you."

"What?"

"I'll marry you, Finn."

"Yeah?"

She nods.

I pepper kisses on her cheeks, her lips, her eyes. I will never stop kissing her, loving her, being *hers*. Isabelle frames my face in her hands and urges my face away from hers so she can look me in the eyes.

"I love you, Finnigan." She grins. "But you're on your own when it comes to telling your mother. I refuse to be responsible for the rush of power she feels at being right."

"Yeah, I don't think so. You just agreed to marry me, so I think this'll be good practice for doing things as a team."

Isabelle lets her head fall back and she sighs. "Fine."

"Together Izzy. We get through the hard stuff together."

# EPILOGUE

## ISABELLE

*Three years later...*

"Miss Isabelle, are you sure you don't need help out to your car?"

I look up from my desk to see Shane standing in my doorway. It took some time, and a switch to a different group and counselor, but Shane really put in the work and is doing really well. His deficits, as a result of his service to our country, are still present, but he's learned how to compensate for them, and he's turned into an asset as my assistant.

"I'm sure, Shane." I push up from my office chair, groaning when my back twinges. "Finn is picking me up after getting Mickey from day care."

Shane's gaze drops to my belly and his eyes light up. I've gotten used to his excitement over my pregnancy, especially since I told him I'm carrying twins. His childlike wonder no longer creeps me out as it once did.

"Go ahead," I tell him.

He walks around my desk and flattens his hand on my

belly. At least once a week he wants to feel them kick. Fortunately for Shane, they've been very active today.

"Have you guys picked names yet?" he asks, as he always does.

"Actually, we have." He lifts his head and grins. "You have to promise not to tell anyone if I tell you. We haven't even told our family yet."

"I promise, Miss Isabelle."

Before I can answer, Mickey comes running through the door as fast as only a toddler can, his father on his heels.

"Whoa, partner," Shane says and bends down to get at Mickey's level. "Where's the fire?"

"No fire." Mickey lifts his arms, his way of asking to be picked up. "Mama."

"Mickey," Finn says. "We talked about this, remember? Mama can't pick you up because of your brother and sister."

Mickey stomps his foot and pokes his bottom lip out. "I want Mama!" he shouts.

"Micah Isaiah Walsh," I say firmly and rest my hand on the top of his head. "Mama is right here. And I'll be able to pick you up before you know it. But right now, I need you to be my big boy, okay? Can you do that for me?"

Mickey nods but maintains his temper tantrum stance.

"Thank you." I smile at Finn. "Hi, love. How was your day?"

"It was good. Isaiah and I got the contractors started on the addition. They've assured me it'll be done before those two make their appearance." He nods at my stomach and then glances at Shane. "Did you tell him yet?"

"I was just about to."

"Tell me what?" Shane asks excitedly.

"The names of the twins," I remind him.

"Yes, I wanna know."

"We settled on Hank, after my dad," Finn says. "And Hanna. Hank and Hanna."

"Hank and Hanna," Shane repeats as if testing out the names. "I like em'."

"And I'm Micah," Mickey says, tugging on Shane's shirt. "After Pap. Micah, Hank, and Hanna."

"That's right, little man," Finn says and then looks at me. "You about ready to go?"

I brace my hand on my lower back. "More than ready."

"I'll shut everything down, Miss Isabelle. Go home and relax."

"Thank you, Shane."

"You're welcome."

Finn grabs Mickey's hand and throws an arm around my shoulders and leads us outside. Our Jeep is sitting by the curb, waiting for us. I wish it were a Harley. I miss riding. I miss holding onto Finn as we cruise the rural roads, savoring the freedom. But it's not gone forever. Only while I'm pregnant.

"Mom asked if we could stop by the store and pick up some honey glazed carrots for her. She's making her Irish stew and apparently, you used the last bag we had the last time you made it."

"That's because I made it a week ago." I chuckle.

Margaret was true to her word and taught me the recipe. Finn has been grateful for that little cooking lesson ever since.

"Yeah, I know. But I don't have the heart to tell her that."

I wave my hand. "Fine. So much for 'together'," I grumble.

"Do you want to tell her that she can't make her Irish stew because we just had it?"

"Of course not," I laugh.

"I'll tell Grammy," Mickey says from his car seat in the back.

"No!" Finn and I yell simultaneously. "It'll be our little secret, okay?" I tell him.

"Okay, Mama."

Finn pulls away from the curb and navigates the parking lot until he reaches the main

road. I let my head fall against the seat and my eyes drift closed.

"Oh, I forgot to tell you," Finn says. I open my eyes and look at him. "Carson called earlier today. He got the invitation for Mickey's birthday party. He and little Carson will be there."

"That's wonderful."

After Ann died, the Brotherhood retrieved little Carson from Ann's friend's house, where she'd been leaving him for long stretches of time. We also took all of the evidence we'd gathered about her to an attorney and retained him for Carson so he could get his son back. It took several months and a lot of money, but it was worth it.

"He even asked if he could bring someone," Finn adds. "I guess he's dating a woman who has a son about the same age as little Carson. I told him that was fine." He looks at me. "I hope that's okay."

"Of course it is."

Finn reaches across the center console and lifts my hand into his. "I love you, Izzy." He brings my hand to his lips and gently kisses it. "I love you and Mickey and Hank and Hanna and the life we've built."

"I love you too, Finn."

Finn pulls into the grocery store parking lot and runs in to grab the carrots for his mother. Mickey remains in his car seat, singing his ABCs and being generally silly. When Finn comes back out, I allow my eyes to fall closed again and let the drive home lull me to sleep.

"Izzy."

I come awake with a start. "What?" I look around. "We're home already?"

"You sweep, Mama," Mickey chortles.

"I guess I did."

I twist to open my car door, but Finn stops me with a hand on my arm.

"What is it?" I ask over my shoulder.

He shakes his head, his eyes suspiciously shiny. "Nothing. I just… Thank you."

"For what?"

"Everything. For giving me everything."

# A NOTE FROM ANDI

I want to start off by thanking you for reading Broken Loyalty. Without you, the readers, the Broken Rebel Brotherhood wouldn't have gone on as long as they have.

It has been a long journey with these characters, one that I will always cherish. They were the first characters to make themselves known in my head, the first to demand I tell their stories. But they certainly won't be the last!

As I close this particular chapter in my writing journey, I embrace the excitement for what's to come. And I hope that you will stay on this road with me for the rest of the ride.

I also want to take a minute to give a huge shoutout to those who have stood by me since the day I walked in the door and announced I was going to write a book.

My husband, Andy, has been my biggest supporter and my loudest cheerleader. He has not doubted me for a single second, even when I doubt myself.

My best friend, Courtney, has been with me on this journey from day one. Our friendship started out as a random message on Facebook about potentially becoming critique partners and has blossomed into a friendship that I cherish more than words can say. We may live hundreds of miles apart but she's always there, no questions asked. She is my person and without her, I wouldn't have made it this far.

My PA and one of my closest friends, Darcie, started out as a reader and morphed into one of the most important people in my life. Without her, I probably would have killed some characters off so make sure you thank her!!

My parents and sister have cheered me on from the sidelines for as long as I can remember. They've believed in me even when I didn't believe in myself. They're forever saying 'You've got this' and for that, there are no words.

I know there are individuals I have likely missed and for that I apologize. It wasn't my intention to have this turn into a Oscar-like acceptance speech but I also believe in acknowledging those who have helped shape me into, not only the person I am, but the author that I am.

Thank you all so very much for supporting me, believing in me, and for reading my books. As long as there are readers who want more, I will create more!

Much love,

Andi

# ABOUT THE AUTHOR

 Andi Rhodes is an author whose passion is creating romance from chaos in all her books! She writes MC (motorcycle club) romance with a generous helping of suspense and doesn't shy away from the more difficult topics. Her books can be triggering for some so consider yourself warned. Andi also ensures each book ends with the couple getting their HEA! Most importantly, Andi is living her real life HEA with her husband and their boxers.

For access to release info, updates, and exclusive content, be sure to sign up for Andi's newsletter at andirhodes.com.

# ALSO BY ANDI RHODES

**Broken Rebel Brotherhood**

Broken Souls

Broken Innocence

Broken Boundaries

Broken Rebel Brotherhood: Complete Series Box set

**Broken Rebel Brotherhood: Next Generation**

Broken Hearts

Broken Wings

Broken Mind

**Bastards and Badges**

Stark Revenge

Slade's Fall

Jett's Guard

**Soulless Kings MC**

Fender

Joker

Piston

Greaser

Riker

Trainwreck

Squirrel

Gibson

**Satan's Legacy MC**

Snow's Angel

Toga's Demons

Magic's Torment

Printed in Great Britain
by Amazon

46787443R00128